Appelfeld, Aharon   cl

Unto the soul

D1490696

UNTO THE SOUL

UNTO THE SOUL

Aharon Appelfeld

Translated from the Hebrew
by Jeffrey M. Green

SCHOCKEN BOOKS

NEW YORK

Copyright © 1994 by Aharon Appelfeld

All rights reserved under International and Pan-American Copyright
Conventions. Published in the United States by Schocken Books Inc., New York,
and simultaneously in Canada by Random House of Canada Limited,
Toronto. Distributed by Pantheon Books, a division of Random House, Inc.,
New York. Originally published in the United States in hardcover by
Random House, Inc., New York, in 1994.

SCHOCKEN and colophon are trademarks of Schocken Books Inc.

Library of Congress Cataloging-in-Publication Data

Appelfeld, Aron.
Unto the soul / Aharon Appelfeld;
translated from the Hebrew by Jeffrey M. Green.
p. cm.
Previously published: New York : Random House, c1994.
ISBN 0-8052-1097-0
1. Jews—Europe, Eastern—History—20th century—Fiction.
2. Brothers and sisters—Europe, Eastern—Fiction.
3. Cemetery managers—Europe, Eastern—Fiction.
4. Jewish families—Europe, Eastern—Fiction.
5. Europe, Eastern—Fiction.
I. Green, Yaacov Jeffrey. II. Title.
PJ5054.A755U94 1998 892.4'36—dc21 97-28619 CIP

Random House Web Address: http://www.randomhouse.com

Printed in the United States of America

First Schocken Paperback Edition 1998

2 4 6 8 9 7 5 3 1

UNTO THE SOUL

It was evening. Amalia stood next to the window. It had been months since the horizon had been so red; torrents of fire, all shades of fire, flowed thickly into the dark mouth of the valley. It was a splendid sight, and Amalia did not budge from the window until the sheets of fire went dark and plunged into the abyss.

Afterward there was silence, and not a sound could be heard in the house. Amalia buried her face in both hands as though trying to store the sight within herself. For a moment it seemed she would sit like that until the day was extinguished and darkness enveloped the house and the courtyard. That was only appearance: her body steadily shrank, and suddenly, with no warning, she burst into tears, heavy sobbing that rose up from within her and made her tremble.

"What's the matter?" her brother cried out.

Upon hearing those words her body shrank even more, and she sank to the floor.

"What's the matter?" He leaned over her.

"I'm frightened."

"Of what?"

"I don't know."

"Nothing's the matter."

"I'm afraid."

"Get hold of yourself."

She raised her head, opened her eyes, and said, "I couldn't control it."

"What?"

"Fear."

"You mustn't fear."

"I won't cry anymore," she said and stifled her voice. Her weeping subsided, and she sat down. He could feel the trembling of her body and her breathing. Like last fall, this time too he spoke of the need to overcome dreads and fears, to gird oneself in order to struggle with the approaching snow and frost.

"Sorry," she said and cut off his talk.

"I don't understand what you're afraid of."

"Of the house."

"Houses are the same everywhere."

"It's different here."

"That's how it seems to you."

He rose to his feet, walked over to the lantern, and lit it. The light revealed her disheveled face. Now he noticed: the narrow blemish over her right eyebrow, which he had loved to look at since his childhood, seemed to have yellowed a little.

"Will it be cold this winter?" she asked, awakened.

"I would assume so, but there's nothing to worry about. The storeroom is full of firewood, and if it's necessary we'll light the other stove too. It'll be as hot as a Turkish bath." Upon hearing his last words, a smile lit her face, and a few of the old lines of beauty came back to it.

"You're too fearful," he chided her gently.

"I know, but what can I do?"

He rose and, without saying anything, went outside. The darkness was greater than he had expected. The horizon was covered with heavy stains of obscurity. He groped his way into the storeroom to light the lantern. This was what he did every night, but tonight, maybe because Amalia had cried, everything seemed narrow and threatening to him. If it weren't dark, he would have gone down to the gentile tavern to have a few drinks. The smells of vodka mixed with human sweat and animal manure calmed him, and he came back from there a new man. Amalia wasn't pleased when he went there, and for that reason he did it on the sly. Sometimes he would run into a gentile woman on the way and spend an hour or two with her. The gentile women in the mountains don't pretend to be faithful. If a man comes their way, they lie with him. When he came back, Amalia would know by the look on his face and the smell of his garments that he had been down at the tavern, not buying supplies. Of course, that infuriated her, and she would torment him insidiously.

Now the autumn was coming with quick steps, and those

pleasures too would no longer be available. Low clouds would dwell on the windows and shutter them.

Only a month ago the place had been buzzing with people, not many but very much in evidence. He knew them by name, by their height, and by their gait. They didn't stay more than three or four days. Still, something of their essence remained. Only the long and tense days of winter erased them little by little from memory. Autumn here was long and turbid. It didn't allow people to leave their houses, nor were their houses secure. The winds tried to knock them down.

Two years ago the autumn had been mild, and memories had spread through the heated house and filled it with sights and shadows. Amalia had evoked forgotten details of her childhood. For some reason her memory had clung to her father, a tall thin man, whose existence had not been felt at home during his life, nor had his death made a strong impression. It was as though he had been an uninvited guest in this world. She had cried for her father a great deal that winter, as though she had just learned of his death by hearsay.

The thought that from now on the place would be empty, and only he and Amalia would be imprisoned in this wasteland, that thought compressed his chest for a moment and stopped his breathing. He was hesitant to return home. Now, very clearly, he remembered the sunset that had burned in the heavens and Amalia's astonished face. A kind of fear seeped into his soul. Everything is illusion; he remembered the old man's voice. He had stayed here for several days, a tall man with a noble face, whose whole height, from his shoes to his cap, had bespoken despair. In all his years of service here he had seen many faces, faces of sadness and faces of distress, but he had never encountered such despair as that old man's. A few times he had tried to approach the old man, but he had repulsed all closeness, and the day everyone had gone down, he too had descended.

When he came home, Amalia was already busy, with body and soul, lugging sacks of potatoes down to the cellar. Both her arms clutched the sacks with the hardworking tenacity of a beast of burden.

"Why didn't you wait for me?"

"The sacks aren't heavy," she answered promptly.

"You could fall down in the dark."

"I'm being careful," she said and continued on her way.

Gad, for some reason, didn't help her this time, and she dragged the sacks efficiently. Finally, she grasped a crate of apples with both hands and carried it downstairs too. The house filled with the odor of mold.

You have to close the cellar door, he was about to tell her, but he didn't say it.

After she finished taking down the sacks and crates, she wiped the sweat from her brow and said, "We have four sacks of potatoes. That will be enough for us, it seems to me." Her full face, sweat-covered, expressed the wonderment of someone who tills the soil.

"We have a few more apples on the trees," he said.

Amalia didn't react. She sat down.

The stove thundered and gave off winter heat. The hunger that had plagued him just a few moments before grew milder. Fatigue enveloped him.

"Why don't we have a cup of coffee?" he said, nevertheless.

"I don't want anything," she said, without moving her hands.

They sat that way for a long while. She was on the couch next to the stove, and he was opposite her on a narrow bench. The wood in the stove was dry and gave off a pleasant warmth. The whole day, the toils and the fears, seemed to fall at their feet. They were too tired to worry or be afraid. So, wordlessly, they both sank down and fell asleep.

CHAPTER 2

The next day Gad rose while it was still dark. The coals hissed in the stove, and the shadows of the flames nestled by Amalia's couch. Amalia herself was still deep in sleep. Seeing her face on the pillow, he remembered the day before with a different clarity. Yesterday, it seemed, he had done nothing but look at the splendors of the sunset. But, miraculously, now he felt no pain. His limbs were calm and his vision was clear.

He immediately went down to the courtyard. The dogs greeted him with yips of joy, and he hurried to give them the leftovers he had kept in the pantry for them. The dogs were famished, and their rounded, sturdy bodies trembled with great hunger. He liked being close to them in the morning.

In the barn a lot of work awaited him. At first that had been Amalia's preserve. She had taken care of the cow and milked it. But since the day she had come upon thieves, she was afraid of the barn. More than once he had reprimanded her, and more than once he had forced her to go out. Indeed, she had obeyed him and gone out, but one morning she returned to the house, her face as white as chalk and her hands dripping with blood. It turned out that the cow had moved sidewards and knocked her over. She sat on the couch for about two hours as though paralyzed. Later she had burst into tears. It was a discordant sobbing that had frightened him and shocked him too. Since then the barn too was his dominion. Now he wasn't sorry, or resentful. He liked that submissive animal, which spread warmth about it and offered gratitude that people tended it and gave it fodder.

In the mild seasons he would take the cow out to pasture. The early morning hours spent with it were hours of quiet pleasure. At the end of summer, they would go as far as the neglected gentile cemetery. From those peaks the landscape was even more open, all sky. Once he had taken Amalia with him there, but she had recoiled at the height and the steepness, and she had not returned.

Meanwhile Amalia arose and prepared breakfast. Gad was glad to see her and said, "Good. How did you sleep?"

"I dreamt about our house in Zhadova all night long."

"And how is it there?"

"The way we left it."

"I didn't dream," he said curtly.

The round loaf of bread stood in the center of the table, and for some reason it reminded him of the summer days that had passed so swiftly. During the summer Amalia would get up early, light the oven, and prepare the dough. Afterward she used to sit some distance away and stare at the flames.

"Is it cold out?"

"The wind is scattering the clouds, and at noon we'll have some sun."

"The clouds make me feel melancholy."

"You mustn't talk that way."

Gad sat in his place. Contact with the hungry dogs and the chores in the barn had whetted his appetite. On the table, alongside the bread, there were two cheese pies that Amalia had prepared the day before in the cellar, a jug of cream, and some onions. During the summer she generally forgot their home on the Plain; the thought crossed his mind. He immediately heaped his plate high with all the good food and dug into it.

Amalia sat at his side and didn't utter a sound. Years ago they used to sit there and converse. Amalia would tell stories, and Gad would listen. Since her childhood she had loved to ornament her speech with fabulous words or words she invented, and in general she had a vocabulary of her own, so that people used to find it difficult to understand her. But that very strangeness charmed him. She wouldn't say "sky," but rather "firmament"; not "curtain," but "veil." At first people thought she was a reader of books, but that was an error, of course. Since her childhood she had liked to collect strange words. In time, as she grew up, her mother had found fault with that habit, and she had scolded her. "Talk like everybody else, or no one will understand you." When her scolding proved useless, she had slapped Amalia's face, and, indeed, the girl stopped saying strange words. In fact, she stopped talking altogether, and her mother wasn't pleased with that either. "People will think you're a mute." But the scolding did no good. Her silences grew stronger year by year. When she was forced to pronounce a sentence, her face would turn red as a beet. Gad hoped the mountain would give back her tongue. Indeed, during the first years she did speak: she told stories, she described things, and sometimes she dropped in an unusual word. None of this lasted very long, and once again she lapsed into muteness.

"Why don't you talk? People will come in the summer, and you'll have to talk to them." He didn't know that a change had taken place in himself. His tongue began to cling to the roof of his mouth, and every time he tried to say something, he choked. Nevertheless, he never ceased demanding of Amalia something that he himself found difficult. For hours they used to sit at the table or next to the window and keep silence.

"We mustn't fall into melancholy. All the Sages warn us against that scourge." He was roused from his thoughts.

"I'm trying very hard," she answered immediately.

"That isn't enough. You have to make an effort."

"What must I do?"

"Don't think about the Plain. We, thank the Lord, have an important task here. We are guarding this holy place, and by virtue of that, no harm will come to us."

"I don't think so."

"It seems to me you're always sunk in nostalgia."

"No," she said. "No."

When they had been down below, he had never criticized

her or pestered her, but here, for some reason, he sometimes felt the need to chide her or preach to her. Amalia did not contradict him or point out his mistakes, perhaps because she understood that his reproaches ultimately were directed at himself, too. He would sometimes sink into his thoughts as though he had been deprived of his will. More than once she had wanted to rouse him and argue about the things he had said to her, but of course she didn't dare.

And thus the days passed, month after month, and again it was autumn. Autumn here lacked beauty. The clouds weighed down from the morning, and in the afternoon, darkness congealed around the windows. But harder than everything was the night. The night was long and sank under the weight of darkness. Often Gad woke up like a drowning man pulling himself out of the sea's undertow. Unlike him, Amalia used to sink into sleep like a stone, and not until late morning would entreaties and threats restore her to this world.

When she got out of bed she would go out to Mauzy and Limzy. From childhood she had loved animals, with a devoted, close love, and they, for their part, returned it sevenfold. Here too she had immediately befriended the dogs. She used to romp with them in the courtyard, but she especially loved to lie down with them in front of the stove and look at the flames. Sometimes they used to fall asleep, intertwined with one another, like a mother and her cubs.

Gad used to be incensed, and often he reproached her. "You spend too much time with the dogs. According to Jewish law it's forbidden to touch dogs." Mauzy and Limzy weren't cuddly dogs. People were petrified of them, and in the summer when pilgrims frequented the place, Gad used to lock them in the shed. A few years ago one of them had slipped away from Amalia and fallen upon a pilgrim. Had it not been for Gad, it's doubtful the man would have escaped from his claws alive. Since then his warnings had been more explicit: You mustn't spend time with the dogs. Amalia would respond by lowering her head or with a smile that smacked somewhat of deceit.

She used to complain about the isolation from time to time.

"We lack nothing," he would interrupt her.

"I get dizzy."

Because you sleep all day, he wanted to say, but he didn't.

Gad arose while it was still fully dark. He would milk the cow and feed it, and then he would immediately come back and light the oven. Formerly he had forced himself to pray, but the effort had given him severe headaches. Amalia, who knew his distress, once said to him, "If praying hurts you, that means you mustn't pray. In the summer men will come, and you'll pray with them." In that way she rescued him from his distress. He would get up in the dark and immedi-

ately go out to do his work. The work occupied his day and
didn't leave him time for thought. Secretly he would console
himself that he was guarding a holy place, and by virtue of
that he would be spared a strict accounting. For hours he
would work in the cemetery, pulling out weeds and righting
tombstones. In autumn there was more work: the furious
rains would sweep away trees and stones without distinction,
and had it not been for the terraces and drainage canals, everything would have been inundated. In the autumn he would
spend most of the day in the cemetery, returning to the house
at nightfall.

Just a month ago, everything had been different. In the
summer they worked together from morning until late at
night. Gad was busy with the people, and Amalia with the
house. The pilgrims were bitter, anguished, and easily angered, but Gad would win them over. They brought him the
mild fragrance of the Plain, human voices, forgotten prayers,
and melodies pleasant to the ear. Hearing their voices he realized how isolated he was, far from the tombs of his parents
and from his childhood friends, who owned stores and ware-
houses and often traveled to the big cities.

Five years earlier he and Amalia had inherited the house
from their Uncle Arieh. Uncle Arieh had invited them up to
the mountaintop, or to his fortress, as he called it. He had led
them from place to place and shown them the graveyard,
which everyone called the Cemetery of the Martyrs, may the
Lord avenge their blood. He had said to them, "I leave in
your hands, children, this holy inheritance. You must watch
over it like the apple of your eye. If you guard it faithfully,

you will lack for nothing. Many people come here, and they will give you everything. You must demand it of them. You mustn't be bashful and silent. They aren't giving you money for nothing. The winter here is long and hard, and except for the crows, there's not a living soul. You need a lot of faith to avoid lapsing into melancholy. Melancholy is the most implacable of opponents. You may take two or three drinks, no more.'' Earthiness imbued Uncle Arieh's ways. At the age of ninety he savored a good meal like a young man.

For a week they had stayed in his company. He had not exaggerated the virtues of the place. He had praised the good air, the large apples and pears on the mountain slopes. He mentioned the faithful dogs and, of course, the house, which had four spacious rooms in which he lodged the pilgrims who had the wherewithal. He spoke about the details but refrained from generalizations, like a man bequeathing a great estate to his son, so he can withdraw and find repose in a smaller residence, far from the highways and daily business. No slacking or confusion was noticeable in him. At the end of the week he shut his eyes and returned his soul to the Creator. That very day he was buried with his fathers. All the pilgrims had taken part in the funeral that evening. The eulogists had spoken of his loyalty and devotion for sixty years without interruption. The women had wept. Late at night one of the old men had spoken in praise of his power to withstand solitude. It was all by virtue of his faith, which had been no less than the faith of his father, who, like him, had lived for many years. But he hadn't been privileged to have a large funeral, for he had died during the winter.

Thus, almost without their noticing it, the mountaintop had fallen to their lot. After the funeral Gad had been deeply moved. In a burst of emotion he swore to observe the proper times for prayer, to immerse himself in the ritual bath, and to study the Mishnah. Amalia's face seemed to grow rounder, like someone who was caught in the wrong place.

"From now on we're here," he proclaimed formally.

"And we won't go back down?"

"It would seem not. What is there down below?"

Thus life had begun here. During the first winter they had felt in their flesh the silence and darkness that padded the house like fluff. Amalia had been seized with excitement and had spoken. Once again she had used the strange words she used to speak in her childhood, and Gad had taken pleasure in them as in an unexpected gift. Gad had been drawn after her and had spoken of the need to free themselves from dense crowding, from pressure, and from outward prayers that sweep away one's awareness. Then, in great enthusiasm, he had promised Amalia that the pure air would do marvels. Amalia had opened her eyes wide and said she was anxiously awaiting them. A kind of childish wonder had been in her face. So pure was the wonder, for a moment it seemed to him that he was deceiving her.

Afterward the long years had come, mainly dark. The summer was merely the wink of an eye. The darkness returned at regular intervals. There were no surprises except those that came from within.

"When will we go back?" Amalia would sometimes rouse from her visions.

"Where?"

"Home."

"We have no home. This is our home. What's wrong with this? We have everything." It sounded like the consolation offered to prisoners when the sunset touches the bars of their cells and the heart perishes with longing.

They had been up there for six years now. Had it not been for the summer, his life would have been even more restricted. The thought that people would come during the summer and fill the barren mountaintop with their bustle: that was the thought which inspired him to act, and on the strength of which he tormented Amalia and told her she mustn't sink into sadness. Within him he knew it would be good if she went down to the Plain, married, and brought children into the world. A number of times they spoke about that, mainly in a truncated way and never explicitly. Upon hearing him her face would round into a smile, as though he were talking of something forbidden.

"Do you miss Zhadova?" He would occasionally press her.

"A little, but it will pass."

She would compress her yearnings within her large breast, and her breast swelled from year to year, testifying with the force of a hundred witnesses that she needed a man and children to suckle. Without these, her body would be corrupted and her wits would be addled. From his own soul he knew her darkness, but he didn't dare suggest that she descend. True, a few of the pilgrims had set their sights on her, and a couple of brazen ones had dared speak to her directly, but she had recoiled and hadn't answered anyone favorably. Speaking had always come hard to her. Now, upon the mountain, it was seven times harder.

During the last summer a pilgrim had attached himself to her, a man of about forty, and he had proposed that she go down to the Plain with him. Gad had found them sitting on the stone step and talking. For the first time since their arrival he had seen her sitting in someone's company, and from a distance she had seemed content. For a moment he was about to walk past them, but the evil spirit within him burst out of his mouth, and he said, "The rooms haven't been tidied, there's nothing in the kitchen, and you're sitting there as if we had servants. If we don't do it, no one will do it for us." Amalia was startled, and with the urgent haste of a hunted animal she returned to the house. That was just momentary anger, and he had forgotten about it, but now he remembered the man's face again, and, as though by chance, he asked, "What did that man want of you?"

"What are you talking about?" She was astonished.

"The man who was talking with you."

Amalia's face turned red, and she said, "He asked for my hand."

•

"Why didn't you tell me?"

"I don't know."

"Did he please you?"

"Not especially."

"What did you tell him?" He asked again one evening.

"I didn't say anything to him."

"What were you talking about?"

"He was talking."

Later he said, "If you want to go down, tell me. I won't stop you. I can live alone here."

"I'm content here," she said.

"I'd like you to get married." He spoke with an elder brother's voice.

"That time has passed, it seems to me."

"You're wrong. I've seen older women than you who got married and had children."

"I'm content here," she repeated.

Late in the afternoon he worked in the cemetery. He pulled out weeds and straightened some gravestones. The light was soft and, without his noticing, evoked the faces of the people who had been there only a few weeks earlier. "They're there and I'm here," he said distractedly. Hidden longings for people once again flooded him and, with them, an oppressive feeling that rose up by itself and gripped the body all about. Now he knew: the summer had died as though it had never been. No one else would come. Amalia would blunt her anger with a few drinks, but not a word would grow up in this wasteland. Formerly he had hoped he would manage to make her talk and they would sit and converse with each other like friends. Now he knew: muteness already stood at the door. Without his noticing it, his Uncle Arieh's face rose up before him. Not a day passed but that he thought about him. Two days before his death he had led Gad to the peak near the abandoned Christian cemetery and told him, as though in secret, "There is no place more beautiful." He spoke with a kind of simplicity, as though he had just discovered it. In Zhadova they had spoken of Uncle Arieh with admiration, but in time that admiration had become tinged with a kind of suspicion that his life was not all that it seemed. But those who had come up here and been saved spoke of him with glowing faces, as though he were part of their salvation. Of the horrors that had been committed here several generations ago, he did not speak. Uncle Arieh had not wanted to talk of it. "The Martyrs," he used to say, "may the Lord avenge their blood, left the world as though with drawn swords." After his wife's death he had come here. He had still been a young man. Since then, sixty years of uninterrupted isolation. Strange, he never mentioned Zhadova except by chance, as though he had never been there.

Nor did Gad tell Amalia what had taken place there. He told her only this: Our grandfather's grandfather, Simha Ber, was among the martyrs. His tombstone was a small, slender one, planed down by the years and by rain, standing in the middle of the cemetery. Amalia used to come and prostrate herself on his grave during the penitential month of Elul.

As Gad stood in the open, a kind of sudden dread gripped him. There was nothing. The sun glided over the clouds, and the evening was near. But there was no darkness yet. Below, on the crests close to the plateau, as always, sheep were scattered. Wagons rolled along lazily as the peasants returned home on paths between the fields. A kind of serenity rose up thickly from the green meadows. But to him, for some reason, it seemed that in a short while a dreadful scream would be heard. He took up the hoe and hurriedly turned in the direction of the house. "No one will save us in our hour of distress." A reflection flitted through his mind, and he hastened his steps.

He found Amalia next to the window, a drink in her hand. "I had a sudden urge for a drink," she said.

"I'll join you. That bottle was brought to us by a Jew from Kolomay. I didn't want to accept it from him, but he wouldn't give in. Everybody feels sorry for us. They don't know that these isolated places have beauty."

"True," said Amalia and opened her eyes.

"Also some hidden power."

"I'm a little bit frightened."

After a few drinks he grew excited and spoke very emotionally about the cemetery, calling it a precious graveyard, which closed its gates before no one.

Amalia was astonished by his words and didn't take her eyes off him. For some reason it seemed to her he had grown older during the past few days, and now he looked a little like Uncle Arieh, and the hidden affection she had secretly harbored for her older brother since her childhood surged up with pity in her, and she said, "You're working too hard."

"You're mistaken, my dear." He spoke to her softly. "I'm barely doing my duty. I have to do more."

"You get up very early."

"I'm not working hard. Believe me. This place gives us

more than we deserve. We have plenty of fruit and vegetables, a roomy house, and firewood for heat. Below people are freezing, but we, thank the Lord, lack nothing. We are protected on every side.''

''And the peasants won't do us any harm?'' She touched upon his hidden dread.

''What are you talking about? We're protected on every side. The peasants down below know very well who is protecting us.''

''Sorry. I'm always frightened.''

''We've been up here for six years. Has anyone ever done us any harm?''

Later, silence fell upon them. Gad, indeed, tried to revive the conversation, but he only managed a few stammers and a couple of sentences whose meaning Amalia didn't catch. Gad kept drinking, and Amalia didn't comment to him about it. Now she sat and observed him, as though expecting some word that would light up her darkness.

CHAPTER 5

Later the rains slashed down and shut them into the house. Amalia worked in the cellar, sorting vegetables and churning butter, and when she came up from there, the smell of moist earth wafted from her clothing. Gad was busy repairing the attic. Contact with the wooden planks brought forgotten odors of home to his nostrils. Now the Plain seemed to him an obscure realm, detached from his life. Sometimes it occurred to him that one day he could rent a wagon and return to Zhadova. Once he had even dreamt that he and Amalia were riding on two bright horses, galloping across fields and reaching their native city. Everyone came outdoors and stood in amazement. In his heart he knew that he would never abandon the peak. A secret covenant had been sworn between the peak and its guardians, a stern covenant, unwritten, passed on from generation to generation.

Up to now no one had ever left. They had all died on the mountaintop, and they were buried in the last row, which was called "the Guardians' Row." Uncle Arieh was buried in that row, and when the day came they would bury Gad there too. If Amalia married and had children, they would come and carry on the dynasty. Sometimes it occurred to him that if he insisted strongly enough, she would marry. If he could write, he would have written to her at great length.

Toward evening Amalia came up from the cellar and made two corn pies, one filled with cheese and one with plums, and they huddled close to the table next to the window and ate. Gad liked those pies a lot. Since morning he had been yearning for them. After the meal he closed his eyes and sang a lullaby, a song full of longing, bringing another sort of sadness from distant parts. Since childhood, she had liked to hear his voice, and now, as he sat at the table, it seemed to her that he was filling her with secrets.

During that season he hardly spoke, just a word here and there, remnants of his speech. Even after a drink, talk was hard for him, not to mention prayer. Since the people had left the place he had not prayed. He very much wanted to pray, but every time he prepared himself to stand up and do so, the words caught in his throat. Two years earlier, on a dark night, he had tried to say a sentence to Amalia, and he had choked. Greatly angry, he had pounded his head against the wall. Finally the obstruction had been torn from his throat, and he had said, "How is it that all Jews pray, and it's hard only for me?"

"You pray in another way." She tried to comfort him.

"That isn't so."

"You watch over this holy place." The words fell into her mouth.

Gad chuckled, and his laughter echoed alarmingly.

"Did I say something silly?" she said and fell silent.

Afterward the rain stopped and the evening opened up. Amalia gathered the things from the table with quiet, restrained movements. Gad rose from his seat and went outside. On his way to the cemetery he stopped for a moment next to the bare acacia tree. Amalia's movements appeared clumsier to him for some reason, as though she were trying to hide a sack of potatoes underneath the bed.

When he reached the cemetery, he forgot everything. He was glad the rains hadn't damaged the tombstones. The drainage canals he had dug in time had borne off the water well. The tombstones projected up over the raised hillock. Gad knew every grave. The saints lay in three rows, in the first row the men, in the second the children, and in the third the women. At some distance, the row of the guardians. Once he had asked Uncle Arieh the meaning of that arrangement, and his uncle had not given him a clear reply. Nor did anyone else know the reason. Now he no longer sought the meaning. The hours here were the loveliest of the day.

More than once Amalia had reproached him for spending too long in the cemetery, but he had ignored her reproaches. In fact, he didn't stay longer than six or seven hours a day, but those hours inspired sights and visions. Here he sometimes saw his small native city, his father and mother, and his two little brothers, who had died in the great typhus epidemic. In the summer it was different, of course. In the summer the plot was stripped of its blue color and of the silence.

People would prostrate themselves on the graves and shake the stones. Sobs were raised up without shame, and whenever a woman fainted, the people around her would carry her out.

As he stood there, thirst for a drink assailed him. If it hadn't been evening, he would have gone down to the gentile tavern and sipped two or three drinks. The smell of tobacco mingling with the smell of alcohol would drive away the sadness from within him, but he didn't like it when Amalia reproached him for it.

When he went back in, Amalia's face was red, and the yellow mark shone on her forehead. It was evident she had drunk from the bottle and overdone it.

"What's the matter?" he asked.

"Nothing at all. Everything is fine." She spoke in a voice not her own, a jolly voice.

"I went up there. The drainage canals worked well."

"You worry too much about them," she said, giggling.

You mustn't talk that way, he was about to tell her, but he said nothing.

"In the world to come there are no winters like here. There it's always summer, isn't it?"

"Why are you talking that way?" He tried to hush her.

"Did I say anything bad?" She recoiled.

Now her face was again naked. Her face was full, like a peasant's, and her head was wrapped in a mane of thick hair. When they had come up here six years earlier, her body had been thin. Her hair had been long and well combed. The embroidered blouse that had been a present from her late Aunt Fanka had suited her face. But since then her hips had grown fuller, her breast had swollen, and the youthful spark in her eyes had dimmed. Now she looked like a peasant woman whose husband was serving in the army, and she, in great anger, and in order to blunt her urges, would drink whenever a bottle was available.

"You had too much to drink." He couldn't restrain himself.

"Not a lot." The laughter froze on her face for a moment.

Now, for some reason, he was about to walk over and slap her face. You slap a drunken woman in the face, and she sobers up, the peasants say. He had never hit her. He liked her drunkenness. Sometimes he would let her chatter as much as she liked. Occasionally the fancy words she had used in her childhood would come back to her.

"According to Jewish law it's forbidden to drink too much," he said perfunctorily.

"You're right," she said.

"I'll make you a cup of coffee."

"Thanks," she said with the relieved expression of a pet that knows it has escaped with a light punishment.

He prepared a cup of coffee for her and served it the way one gives a person medicine. She reached out and grasped the cup with both hands.

"You drink too much," he reminded her again.

"What can I do?" she said, smiling. It was a foolish smile that laid bare another stratum of her face.

"You have to overcome it," he said in a coarse way.

Amalia didn't take her hands off the cup. Gad sat next to her and observed her. The closer he observed her, the more her sense of amazement clung to him. Now he noticed: Her long fingers, with the protruding joints, lay in a pose similar to their father's.

Later, without warning, she burst into tears. Gad hurriedly rose from his seat. He leaned over as though about to pick her up.

"It's nothing," she said and fell to her knees.

Her desperate kneeling opened his mouth. He spoke of the need to sanctify themselves, to bear life with pride, to uproot depression from their hearts.

"Pardon me," she said.

"Why are you asking for pardon?"

"I didn't behave properly."

"You behaved properly. Even the holy books permit us to drink a bit so our spirits won't flag. Melancholy is our enemy. That's the ancient serpent with which we struggle day and night. And if a few drinks can drown melancholy, who are we to stop them?"

Upon hearing those words, a smile flashed on her rumpled face. The old smile illuminated it again.

Later he lit the lantern and went out to the shed to fetch some firewood.

CHAPTER 6

The autumn showed the strength of its arms: the wind stormed without letup. Gad tried to distract her and spoke to her with the words they had used at home. The familiar words brought a smile to her face. "I'm not worried," he said. "So long as we have firewood, we have nothing to worry about." And indeed the stove roared from early morning, and its white-hot sides gave off pleasant heat. During the summer Amalia had turned thirty years old. Gad had remembered her birthday, and as a present he had given her an embroidered peasant scarf that he had bought down below. Amalia had laid it across her shoulders and said, "Youth is gone, gone." Since then, he noticed, a new bitterness had spread upon her lips. She worked obsessively from morning until late at night, and when she came up from the cellar her face was gray, like the women who work in closed workshops.

Since childhood she had hidden in the cellar. In Zhadova they had had a long, narrow cellar where she used to flee from their mother's long, harsh arm. After she had grown up, she would still go down there secretly for two or three hours. Then a kind of will to live had flashed in her eyes. Now fat padded her body, and her smile was thin.

"Mother loved you more." She surprised him one evening.

"It just seems that way to you."

"She only threatened you, but she used to beat me."

"You annoyed her. You used strange words."

"You're mistaken."

"So why did she hit you?"

"She hated me."

"You mustn't talk that way. Mother didn't hate her children."

"I was a speck in her eye," she said, pleased at having found the words to reply.

"You're mistaken."

"After the boys died in the epidemic she hated me. Once she told me, 'You're living by virtue of them.' "

"You mustn't hold a person's grief against her."

"She wanted to kill me," she said, smiling.

"You mustn't talk that way." He tried to scold her.

That evening Amalia guzzled about eight drinks, and her mouth, which had been mute for many days, opened up. She spoke in a torrent, mixing the past and the present, recalling forgotten names and reopening old wounds. It was clear: their mother still pursued her.

"You're going too far." He tried to interrupt her words.

"Every word is perfect truth."

"One mustn't say harsh things against the dead. They are there and we are here. We mustn't disturb their rest."

"Why did she wound me so much?"

"You mustn't bear a grudge."

"It pains me."

"We have to find something positive in everyone. It's forbidden to judge anyone until you've walked in his shoes."

"I'm not going to have any children," she said, bursting out laughing. The laughter revealed her strong white teeth.

Gad gulped down a drink, rose to his feet, and said, "The storm has let up outside. I have to see what damage the rains have done to the cemetery. But you, I beg of you, don't drink anymore. Drinking isn't proper for Jews."

Amalia accepted that reproach with a smile. For years now she had wanted to share her secret with him. Now that she had revealed it, she felt relieved. She gathered her hair, and her full face, etched along its breadth with wrinkles from hard work, seemed to open up. For some reason it seemed to him that she wanted to reveal yet another secret to him, graver than the first.

"Do you promise me?" he said.

"What?"

"Not to touch the bottle."

"May I join you?" She surprised him again.

The evening was lit with the dim lights of the cold autumn, and in his heart Gad knew it was forbidden to torment his sister any further. Her wounds were deep, and they should be dressed with a soft bandage.

"Thanks," he said.

"What for?"

"For talking with me. Talk brings one closer, isn't that so?"

"You are my beloved brother," she said and immediately recoiled from the words she had spoken.

Gad chuckled as though his sister had touched his hidden weakness.

When they reached the cemetery, his eyes went dark: the strong rains had weakened the stone wall and knocked down a row of gravestones. At the sight of the flood-washed cemetery a cold groan escaped his mouth, and he said, "Great God, what has been done to us?"

"Who did it?" Amalia was shocked too.

"Can't you see?"

Without delay he rushed to the tombstones, kneeled down, and righted them one by one. Amalia stood nearby and watched him toil. He was immersed in it, as though he was tending sick animals. Once he had wanted to erect a wooden roof over the tombstones to protect them from the winter storms, but the old men rejected his suggestion. One doesn't erect a barrier between heaven and earth, it is said, and thus they erased the cherished thought he had husbanded for many days.

Years had passed since then. Every winter the sky fell upon the earth, flooding, uprooting, and leaving destruction behind. Gad tried to wall in the breaches, to lay buttresses behind the least stable of the gravestones, but they could not withstand the furious rains. At one time he had secretly grumbled against the old men, who had not, as it were, grasped his intention. Now he knew not even a roof would have been effective. The rain would uproot everything, including him. The sadness was palpable now and seeped through all his limbs.

After finishing the work he stood for quite a while. Three years earlier, in the same season, the winds had knocked down many tombstones. He had known it wasn't a good sign. He was sure it had been his fault, but during the summer it became clear: an epidemic of smallpox had spread throughout the region and felled many victims.

"Everything is in place, thank God," said Amalia. Now she knew how attached her brother was to the place, and she pitied him for his devotion and because he had to struggle all winter against the dreadful winds.

On the way back she blurted out a few sentences that sounded like words of consolation. Gad didn't respond. A kind of cloud wrapped his face. He took hurried steps, like someone whose employer has dismissed him.

C H A P T E R   7

The next day, surprisingly, a wanderer appeared on foot, a Jewish peddler, and stood outside.

"What are you doing here?" Gad addressed him the way one addresses a ghostly shadow. Were it not for his short coat, he would have resembled a lost pilgrim, but his cap and his coat showed immediately that he hadn't come to prostrate himself upon the tombs.

"I made a mistake," he said, like someone who had led himself astray.

"Didn't you know the way?" Gad asked in the stranger's tone of voice.

"I knew it, but I still made a mistake," he said, not without accusing himself.

"And now do you know where you are?"

"So it seems."

"You're at the Martyrs', may God avenge their blood."

"Great God!" said the peddler, slapping his forehead. "What have I done?"

It was a gray afternoon, and Amalia served them cups of coffee and bread and butter. She immediately withdrew and went down to the cellar. The peddler recovered himself. Words returned to his tongue. He spoke as peddlers speak, mixing truth and wishful thinking, making things up about places and people. Gad was closely familiar with these frivolous men, but nevertheless he couldn't restrain himself and told him about the solitude and about the dread of winter that had been Uncle Arieh's lot and now had become his own. "If the solitude is hard for me, it's seven times harder for my sister." Inadvertently he revealed his hidden sorrow. While he allowed a glimpse of his pain, he regretted his words, changed his tone, and said, "How are things down below?"

"The world hasn't changed; everything's rotten."

"Here there are no changes; one year follows the last."

"But at least you make a living."

"Not a fortune." Gad hid nothing from him.

"I'd go away. Let the pilgrims watch." The peddler bared his voice.

"Food isn't lacking." Gad tried to sweeten his words a little.

"A cemetery is no rose garden," said the peddler, and Gad knew he had acquired that figure of speech from the innkeeper on the way, where city people stop over.

"I'm not complaining." Gad gave his remarks a religious tone.

"I'm complaining. About unfairness and injustice. I'm complaining. I don't bear afflictions with love."

Now he noticed that the peddler's face didn't contain even a tiny flash of the fear of heaven. His face was bearded, but its expression was cold and practical. These are the sort who convert easily. The thought flitted through his head.

"How much do they pay you?" The peddler probed.

"Who?"

"The descendants of the martyrs."

"The martyrs now belong to the Jewish people."

"But still, who pays?"

"Whoever has something to give, gives." Now Gad remembered that in the past summer no one had made a real contribution. The alms box had remained empty, and had it not been for the cow, the fruit, and the vegetables, they wouldn't have had anything to eat. Nevertheless he wanted to rise from his seat and say, Not by bread alone does a man live. We, thank God, are prepared to serve the Jewish people even without any recompense. The right to live on this mountain peak can't be reckoned in money. But seeing the peddler's face, a profane face, a face from which faith had been extinguished, with a kind of meagerness spread on his bitter cheeks: seeing these, he stifled his voice within himself and said nothing.

"I would leave this place. Without pay there can be no watch. Never in my life have I seen a free watchman."

"We have property rights to the place."

"Property rights." The peddler repeated the phrase and laughed. "Property rights to the mountain, property rights to the winter, property rights to all the treasures of nature.'' Gad was filled with dread by the man's dissolute voice and lowered his face over his cup. Afterward the peddler asked a few questions, each with a kind of hidden barb to them. Gad was cautious, spoke in general terms, and said nothing specific. The small pleasure he had taken in him progressively dissipated. Oppression gripped his breast.

Gad rose to his feet and said, ''A great deal of work awaits me. I must go.'' He was pleased that he had had the strength to say that without apologizing.

''I wouldn't stay here for one day.'' The peddler spoke cuttingly.

''Everyone has his task in the world.'' Gad employed a saying he had heard.

Upon hearing that sentence the stranger opened his eyes, big round eyes, in which a kind of naked dampness sparkled, and he said, ''I don't sell merchandise on credit. I demand immediate payment.''

Gad didn't grasp the enormity of his response, and when he did grasp it, a tremor passed over his spine.

''We'll certainly see each other again.'' Gad tried to distance himself from the man.

''Not in this place.''

''Where?'' His tongue impelled him to ask.

''Down below. Only down below. Down below they pay for work and for merchandise. Down below there are no free watchmen. Everybody knows his place. There are no illusions. In the future I won't get lost again. I've learned my lesson,'' said the man, and with youthful steps he turned toward the slope.

In the evening heavy rain fell. Gad sat at the table without uttering a sound. The peddler's short visit had left a kind of searing gloom that soon turned to self-pity. Amalia quickly prepared some vegetable soup and a savory pie with sour cream. She knew only those foods could relieve his depression.

After the meal he announced he had it in mind to go down below and fetch the supplies they would need for the winter. Amalia hated those descents of his. She knew: he let himself have more than one extra drink. But this time she said nothing. Later she said, "I'm afraid to stay alone."

"We can't both go down."

"I'd rather go down and not stay alone."

"By yourself?"

"It's better to meet the wolf than to wait in dread." She spoke the peasants' language.

"I won't permit you to go down by yourself."

"I'm not afraid of the road. I'm afraid of the walls."

"Of the walls?"

"The outdoors doesn't frighten me."

"We mustn't leave the place unattended." He tried another tack. "We swore to Uncle Arieh and to the generations of watchmen before us. Don't you remember?"

"I don't remember. When was that?"

"You don't want to remember."

That was the end of the conversation. Gad filled the stove with dry wood, placed a pot of water over the flame, and drank two cups of coffee one right after the other. It had been months since he'd touched a woman's body. In the spring he had indeed gone down below, visited the tavern, and hoped to meet a woman on the way. But to his misfortune, none had appeared, and the appetite remained in his body like a poison and tormented him with turbid dreams. Later, when Amalia came up from the cellar, she turned to him and said, "I'm at ease in my mind. You can go down."

"How come?"

"I'm not frightened anymore."

"What happened?"

"I overcame my fear."

"I don't understand," he said and immediately regretted misleading her.

The following days were dark, rainy, and cold. Gad lit the two stoves and Amalia didn't remove her old army coat, but despite everything Gad scrupulously tended the cemetery every day, even now. Upon returning home his clothes would be wet, and he would be completely dirty. Amalia would hurriedly hand him a bath towel and dry clothes. At first she rebuked him. "You're liable, God forbid, to come down with pneumonia." But she stopped. She realized his resolve was firm: one mustn't leave the cemetery unattended.

By afternoon the house would already be as dark as a cave, and Gad would light the kerosene lantern and sit at the table, waiting for a bowl of soup. It took two bowls of soup to infuse his body with warmth. Sometimes, distractedly, Amalia would recall sights from her childhood and tell him. Gad said repeatedly that they had to cut themselves off from the Plain.

Thoughts about the Plain aroused bad hopes, and it was better to be occupied with present concerns, to fortify the
house, and to lay in a supply of water and wood. Gad himself
was sometimes caught up in memories, wallowing in them
with a strange pleasure. As time passed it became clear that
the onset of the snows was only a matter of hours. The snow
cut the mountaintop off completely from the roads and the
Plain. Amalia was pleased in her heart that Gad had not gone
to the village. What they had in the storeroom would suffice.
In the storeroom, on shelves, lay a few bottles of oil, hunks of
smoked meat, flour, and sugar. True, in the past year the pilgrims had been stingy, but they still brought something, and
that little bit was added to what remained from the year
before. People had not been generous, but the heavens had.
The summer had been mild, the rains well timed, and the
vegetable beds had produced abundantly. The trees as well
had been laden with fruit. One mustn't trust in people: today
they look upon you pleasantly, and tomorrow they clench
their fists as though obsessed.

In previous years he hadn't kept accounts, but now he said
openly that not only had they stopped making contributions,
they also were registering complaints: the place wasn't properly maintained. Uncle Arieh had been high-handed and severe with the pilgrims, dogging their steps and demanding
substantial contributions. Anyone who slipped away was pub-
licly reviled. "Let everyone know," he used to say, "that
without charity there's no life. Anyone who doesn't give
charity here is like one who murders a soul." And indeed
people gave; they had to. "Prayers are not answered unless
they are accompanied by charity," he used to castigate them.

Gad didn't know how to demand. Because he didn't demand, people stopped giving. After Uncle Arieh's death, awe of him still hovered over the people, but gradually that awe had dissipated. Gad muttered, threatened, and finally decided he would stand at the gate and collect an entrance fee. But not even that stratagem was successful. People snuck in and slipped away.

True, there were also a few, the faithful, who brought what they could afford to give: a canister of oil, a sack of sugar, or a bottle of slivovitz. "If anyone doesn't give, I'll kick him out." He surprised Amalia with his words.

"No," she blurted out.

"I'll do exactly what Uncle Arieh did. I'll kick them out."

In her heart Amalia knew that her brother wouldn't do that. He had neither his uncle's strength nor his faith. Nevertheless, she was afraid to say so.

"The winter is long, and we need food. I won't give in."

Imperceptibly, other things also rose up from the thick of the years. After their parents' death no one had come forward to help them. Their few relations had avoided them, and other people ignored them. Amalia had worked as a housekeeper and Gad as a day laborer in a lumberyard. The work was hard, and they earned a poor living. Strangely, those oppressive memories brought an odd kind of religiosity to her face, but Gad mercilessly laid bare the truth: If our own people hadn't driven us away, we wouldn't be here.

"They didn't mean to drive us away." She tried to find a point in their favor.

"If it hadn't been for Uncle Arieh, we would have starved to death. The Plain is crueler than the mountain. The mountain is cold, but it isn't wicked. The winds knock down trees, but they aren't evil.''

It was clear: he bore a grudge against the Plain in his heart. ''Everyone has his place. I have no regrets. The Plain disgusts me. We, thank God, have open spaces, a different way of seeing and hearing. I wouldn't live there for any price in the world.''

Later, after he had drunk a few drinks, he was aroused and spoke with a different kind of eloquence about a life of devotion and sacrifice of the soul. ''Without spirit the body too degenerates. A ruined body oppresses the soul and blinds its eyes.'' Those were sentences he had absorbed from the old men who used to teach a chapter of some holy book between one prayer service and another, and now, as he repeated them, they sounded like crazy yearning.

''I dreamt about home last night,'' Amalia remembered.

''Whom did you see?''

''I saw Father.''

''And what did you tell him?''

''I promised to visit him. He was pleased by my promise.''

For a moment he was charmed by the look of her face. There were hours during the day when her face was bright and her look was clear and her years didn't show on her. She would be very similar to the little Amalia who used to sit in the yard, as though the years had not passed.

''One day we'll go down,'' he said, almost distractedly.

''When?''

''We have to find a substitute, a faithful substitute. In the summer I'll get advice from one of the old men.''

Hardly had he said the word "substitute" when her face brightened, and she said, "Father will certainly be very glad."

At night, when the rain grew harder, she wanted to let the dogs in. Usually Gad refused to admit them, but this time, for some reason, he agreed. The dogs bounded in and yelped with joy. Gad knew in a short while they would curl up on the floor in front of the fire, and Amalia would sing them an idle Ruthenian song she had heard in her childhood. You mustn't lie on the floor with the dogs, he wanted to call out to her, but the words failed him.

Later he recovered. He sat at her side and spoke of the need to act with severity, to demand substantial contributions from the pilgrims, because the roof was likely to cave in and the fence wasn't stable, either. If he didn't make repairs in time, they would collapse. For a moment it seemed as if he wasn't annoyed with the pilgrims but with himself and his weakness.

"You did everything in good faith and honestly," she said, gathering the dogs up against her body with both arms.

"No, my dear," he said, with a kind of excessive emphasis.

"You're wrong, my dear." She spoke to him softly. "The people are hypocrites. The prayers of someone who prays while unclean won't be answered. If a person wishes to be purified, he is helped from on high. But to come here and avoid responsibility, to steal, not to leave a contribution for the people who stay here in the winter—that's fraud. You can cheat flesh and blood but not heaven."

Gad was amazed by the words and phrases she had spoken. He had not imagined that the old men's reproaches had been absorbed so deeply in her heart.

"Amalia," he said.

"What?"

"You listen to what the old men say, don't you?"

"I love to hear their voices. Sometimes it seems to me that they're speaking with the voice of Greatness."

"I don't understand what you're talking about."

"There's a light in their faces. Didn't you see the light in their faces?"

But later he got very angry because her eyes were red, her hair was disheveled, and she was hugging the dogs with wanton abandon. According to Jewish law, anyone who lies with a beast will be put to death. It's only permitted to love human beings, he wanted to cry out loudly.

"We drank too much, didn't we?" she said.

"How many bottles are left?"

"There's more."

"We have to keep a sharp eye on the drink. We mustn't be left without drink. How much is left?"

"There are six more bottles."

"That's very little."

"You're right."

"If anyone comes without bringing us a bottle, I won't let him cross the threshold."

A kind of drunken rage thickened in his eyes, and it was clear he was about to fall upon the dogs and throw them out. He was going to raise his voice against Amalia and shout, Go to bed. You're not allowed to hug the dogs!

CHAPTER 9

The days grew dimmer as the season advanced. At last storms swept the mountaintop and darkened it. The walls shook from the force of the wind. Every year saw the same frightful spectacle, but nevertheless it was hard to get used to it. Years ago he had been enthusiastic and had swept Amalia away with his emotion. More than once he had been amazed by his words. True, they had not been his own words. Nonetheless, they had a certain strength. And sometimes, when he was very enthusiastic, he would also grasp and understand a word or verse from the Torah, and that would astound him for a moment. However, as time passed, his enthusiasm had progressively faded, not by itself. He tried to inspire his life with patience and faith, but desire for a woman, the darkness of the winter, Amalia's frequent relapses—all these had extinguished the fire bit by bit.

Amalia's face gradually became opaque. She neither complained nor rebuked him, but her entire life was embodied in her indifference. When she relapsed, as she had often done during the past two years, longings, pains, and recriminations would burst out, as from a smoking maw. Their main point was: Why are we tormenting ourselves here? The darkness is devouring us, and our flesh is rotting.

Amalia's rebukes would awaken and inspire him with words. He would chasten and console her until he momentarily blunted her fears. But that ability grew steadily weaker, speech was locked up within him, and even the little that he said would cost him his soul. Only slivovitz, only that and no other strong drink, would briefly open up the channels of his heart.

During the first winter they had already learned to drink. In fact there had been no need to learn. The darkness of the winter had led them to the bottle as to a life raft. At first he had reproached her and proved with signs and wonders that drinking was an original sin and debased man. Meanwhile he too was trapped by excessive liquor. During the winter nights a kind of closeness flamed up between them. He would call her by pet names, and, for her part, she would make provocative gestures and say to him, "But you love the gentile women."

Now came the seventh winter. Henceforth, time was no longer divided into day and night, but everything was a tumultuous river of black snow. In the first years Amalia had suffered severe lapses in this season. She would wrap herself in the army coat and say, "I don't want to see how they shut us up behind locks and bolts."

"What locks and bolts are you talking about?"

He used to sit at her side for hours and try to banish the horrible sights that paralyzed her. But talk was useless. She was sure that at night the winds would strangle her. Then, in the image of a hidden redeemer, the bottle of slivovitz would appear. She would drink and vomit, drink and vomit. In the end, she came to love the bitter liquid. She learned how to sit alone with a bottle and sip from it until she reached oblivion. Gad's path to slivovitz was simpler, perhaps because he had seen how his Uncle Arieh, at the age of ninety, used to swallow a whole glass without batting an eyelash.

"It's coming again," said Amalia, smiling.

"As long as we have firewood, there's nothing to worry about. Let the winds run wild outside. Let them rage. But here we won't let them get a foot in the door." Again he invoked the old answer, worn from frequent use.

"Down below people dress up and go out in the street, don't they?"

"Here too we go out. Between one storm and another there are lulls. They have streets and we have firmaments. This is no prison, my dear."

Amalia opened her large eyes, and, at the same time, they expressed suspicion, sadness, and pain.

"It isn't a prison, thank God. We have everything." He grasped at that straw.

"I promised Father I would visit him. One mustn't break promises."

"We received greetings from Zhadova this year, Haya Bronfman herself," he answered indirectly.

"She frightens me."

"What's the matter?"

"She told me, 'Don't move from here. Down below there are nothing but pogroms and epidemics. Death devours with all its mouth.' I don't understand why she said, 'With all its mouth.' "

He was almost about to say, I told you so, but he restrained himself, and instead he summed up with the following words: "The town is hovering above the jaws of disaster. Anyone who doesn't run away in time is doomed to destruction."

Hearing that dire prediction, Amalia bent her head, and her hair, which had gone gray in the middle of her scalp, stood out all the more.

"Haya Bronfman is a very unfortunate woman, may we be spared her fate. All her offspring died in the great typhus epidemic," Gad said in a tired voice, like someone doing his duty.

"And the epidemic won't reach here?" Amalia asked in a distracted way.

"We have nothing to fear. The air here is clear and pure. Only us, with no barrier." Amalia had never before heard the phrase "with no barrier." It sounded strange to her, as though it came from a doctor's mouth.

"And what about the promise I made to Father?"

"A promise that's impossible to keep is automatically void."

"But what shall I say to him when he appears in a dream again?"

"Don't say anything to him. He'll understand."

Sometimes it seemed to her that if she returned to her native city her life would be cured of all its oppressions and bad dreams, and bright visions would surround her again as in her youth. Several times she had wanted to talk to Gad about that, but she was apprehensive. This time the words came to her, and she said, "I would like to ask forgiveness of Mother. All these years I've borne a grudge against her."

"Why do you recall it now?"

"I saw their graves, and they were neglected."

"We haven't abandoned them. We sometimes think about them."

Later, like an echo from other conversations, he said, "I feel detached from there. A place with a lot of Jews has troubles. There are epidemics and persecutions. I prefer this place. It's isolated."

Upon hearing that answer, Amalia placed both her hands on the table as though to say, I no longer have the strength to struggle.

Now he had a desire once again to lecture her about the advantages of the place and its sanctity. But he remembered that he had already lectured her several times, and it was better to avoid repetition.

"How many years have we been here?" she asked, as though waking up.

"This is the seventh year. Have you already forgotten?"

"It seemed to me this was the eighth year."

"Who would have imagined we'd hold our own here for seven years? When we first came you wept a lot, and I didn't know what to say to you. The winter was dreadful. The walls shook with the power of the wind. We prevailed, thank the Lord. If one has faith, one prevails."

Amalia knew the faith in her heart was progressively shrinking with the passing years, and in the dark hours of the day even that little bit abandoned her, and melancholy took absolute dominion over her. She knew it, but she didn't dare say it. Where is that faith you're talking about? Where is it to be found? This mountain has destroyed me.

Gad knew what her silence meant, and he raised his head and said, "Our faith was never great, nor is it now, but still we have done something. Let that be no small thing in your eyes. Were it not for us, were it not for our seven devoted years, this would not be a place to which people come to pray but just a barren mountaintop. That's no small matter. Someone has to pay."

Later Amalia prepared two pies, one with corn and one with cabbage. Imperceptibly the warm aromas evoked an old and forgotten feeling of home and, in addition, another feeling, frightfully selfish: It's good that we're here, far away from the towns, where not only storms are raging now, but also sicknesses and epidemics.

CHAPTER 10

During the winter month of Kislev the days were as dark as night, and Amalia never crossed the threshold of the house. The dogs howled like wolves. Gad started sawing wood in the shed early in the morning to lay in a supply. Every time he came up from the shed, he would say, "It's good that we're here. In the Plain people are dying from the cold."

The stoves roared indeed. It was difficult to retain the heat, but if they didn't let the fire go out, some of the heat was preserved. As in every Kislev, Amalia sank into a kind of frozen silence. The dark yellow patch on her forehead seemed to sink in, and her cheeks were shrunken and stretched tight. Leave your hands on the table, he wanted to tell her for some reason. Open hands dissolved the dread. But he grasped immediately that his thought was baseless. At night he spoke with her nonetheless about the sadness that devours everything good and darkens the soul. One must extricate oneself from the mud as long as one lives and has the power to do so.

Amalia did not respond. She looked at him with her large, extinguished eyes, as though to say, Why are you tormenting me?

"You mustn't complain," he said, as though she had complained.

In the afternoon he would peel potatoes, dice onions, doing all the housework Amalia was too indolent to do, and they would eat. For hours they would sit and eat. The silent actions of her mouth would give her face the expression of a mute. Sometimes she would fall asleep at the table, her blouse unbuttoned, her mouth puffed up, as though this were not a home but a bustling railroad station where porters loaded bales and kegs and refugees curled up in every corner and slept. Redness spread upon her neck and cheeks like a peasant woman in a tavern.

Thus the month of Kislev passed, the Feast of Lights ignored. The snow fell without letup, and the darkness was great. It was hard to arouse her from her sleep in the morning. Even strong coffee failed. Sleep drew her down as though by strong cords. Only at night a few drinks of slivovitz would rouse her extinguished eyes, and she would smile.

One night he felt that her right leg had crossed over to his bed. First he tried to shove it away, as he did when she snored. Indeed he did push it, but the full leg, extended across the bed, wouldn't move.

"Amalia," he called in a whisper. Years ago, when she had

been about six, she used to sneak into his bed toward morning and tickle his foot. She had apparently guessed that tickling gave him pleasure. After a while their mother had caught her in the act. She had pulled her aside abruptly and slapped her on the face. Amalia had stood, abashed, and had not uttered a word. Their mother, seeing that, had fallen upon her again and beaten her thoroughly. Strange, their mother had not reprimanded her, and Amalia hadn't cried. Perhaps because of that the nightmare had been engraved in his memory. Afterward, although they had slept in the same room, she had not dared approach his bed.

Now Amalia's face was burrowed into the pillow, but the nape of her neck was lit, a broad neck as though planed in both her shoulders. That side of her body had been hidden from him up to now.

When they had first come up to the mountain her figure was thin and long, and a kind of white youthfulness was spread upon her face. The first two winters had changed her beyond recognition. Her body had filled out, her arms had turned red. She looked like one of the peasant women who lived on the nearby peaks. The change that had taken place before his eyes was absolute, but he became used to it, not without being pleased that his sister was no longer a weak creature but a full woman.

While he looked at her she moved somewhat, without changing her position. The stove now lit her shoulders, the concavity above her hip, and her left leg. He knew her left foot well. In childhood she had sprained it several times, and each time they had brought her to the medical station the medic would say, "That wild girl again."

"She isn't wild. She has no luck," said her father, as though to protect her.

"How did it happen?" he would ask with interest.

"She tripped."

"Things like that don't happen right in the street."

"There was a pit."

"That's something else," he would say and immediately go out to fetch splints to set her leg. From the time of his youth Gad had liked to scrutinize that foot, which was so subject to misfortune. It had an airy kind of gracefulness, perhaps because of the short big toe.

He rose from his bed and walked over to the stove. She lay across both of the beds, with her right leg folded up and her left leg extended stiffly, which made the bulge of her buttocks stand out. That is how she had lain since childhood. But this time her way of lying had weight, as though she were attached to the mattress. Move aside, he was about to say. Years ago, when he was already about eleven, he had seen her washing in the bathtub. She was still a girl, but her movements even at that time had been those of a young woman. She had pulled her hair up as though to show the length of her neck. He had liked to look at her, and when she grew up he didn't cease. He would close his eyes so as not to stare at her, but his imagination was stronger than the stare itself.

Now he remembered: when they had come up to the mountaintop, Amalia had shivered and wept, and he had not known what to do. Thoroughly baffled, he had said, "There's nothing to be afraid of. No one will come here. The whole mountain will be ours. Just for us." That last sentence had stopped her weeping, and a kind of youthful wonderment had fluttered upon her face, as though she had seized upon some distant memory. He had given her a cup of tea, and she had drunk without thanking him. Afterward had come six years of fear and of stifled, secret love, memories, and distractions. Hardest of all were the suspicions: Who would betray whom? When her spirits were raised by strong drink, she would say, "You should go down there."

"You're sending me to the gentile women."

"I'm no good. They'll be good to you."

"You're better than they are." Upon hearing those words she would break out in wild laughter, as though he had whispered a vulgarity in her ear.

Now the waters had neared the abyss. He bent to his knees and touched her foot. The foot trembled but didn't move. He pressed his lips upon the hollow of her arch and devoured, bit by bit, the entire length of her body. She didn't even move when he sank his teeth in her neck—as though it had been secretly agreed between them that this is how things would be when the time came.

CHAPTER 11

The next day they slept late. When they woke up, a few bright patches peeked out in the sky, and Amalia's face was flushed and confused. The house had grown cold and Gad quickly fanned up a blaze in the coals. Amalia was in no rush to get out of bed. Gad stood by the window and, with great clarity, remembered the cold winter days at home, the store, and the customers who had stood bundled up next to the cashier, shivering with cold. He remembered his mother's red hands and his father, who used to drag sacks toward the door. Amalia was little, and in the winter they didn't allow her to leave the house. Once she had dared to sneak into the store. When their mother noticed her she came out from behind the counter; with a swift and cruel movement, she snatched her up and slapped her face. She was not content until she had also pinched her. Amalia sobbed, and their mother, extremely angry, had stopped her mouth. Immediately afterward she had returned to the counter and, all at once, wiped the anger from her face and stepped forward to serve the next customer.

"The coffee is on the table," Gad called out in a clear voice.

"I'm coming." The answer was prompt.

Amalia stepped up to the basin, washed her face, and wrapped her head in a kerchief. They sat and drank cup after cup. Gad tried to say a couple of words in a soft voice, but the words came out empty and insipid. Amalia followed every word with a kind of confused tension.

"We have to water the animals." He woke up.

"What time is it?" she asked distractedly.

"Eleven-thirty."

First he gave water to the dogs, and then he went into the barn. The cow, whose master had brought the fodder in late, expressed its discontentment by tilting its head in annoyance. Gad patted its head and immediately set to milking it. Its udders were full, and the milking took a long time.

Contact with the silent animal imperceptibly reminded him of Amalia's illuminated face, of the smell of her armpit and the taste of her breasts.

When he returned to the house with the pail of milk in his hand, Amalia was sitting on the bed, leaning back on both her arms, a pose he had not noticed her in before. A flash of blue sparkled in her gaze, and it seemed she was about to utter some warning.

"I'm going down to cut firewood. Be so good as to put the milk in the pantry." He tried to give his voice a domestic tone.

"Right away." Amalia swung her legs out of bed.

"It's very cold outside." He spoke in his father's voice. He immediately went down and immersed himself in the work. He worked without a pause, and in the afternoon a pile of cut wood stood at the door of the shed. Gad was content with the quality of the wood.

When he came up he noted that she had not prepared lunch. For a moment he was about to scold her, but he stifled his complaint and said, "What shall we cook today? I'm hungry."

"I'm not hungry."

"But you have to eat." He placated her.

"I don't feel like it."

Now he noticed that a self-indulgent tone had crept into her voice. For a moment he was about to approach her and stroke her head, to tell her, Let's cook lunch together. I'll peel the potatoes and dice the onions. Within an hour we'll have a meal. Amalia apparently sensed his intention and chuckled.

Finally he said, "I'll make it." He immediately took two earthenware pots out of the cupboard. He prepared the meal, and Amalia observed him without helping. Gad was excited and spoke like someone who intends to tell a long story. That of course was a misapprehension. After a few sentences his voice got stuck. He tried to continue, and it stuck again. Finally he said, "As soon as the snow melts I intend to build a new fence around the cemetery and to make the drainage canal deeper. Otherwise the rain will sweep away the grave-stones.'' Those few sentences recalled other words within him, not new ones but words he had already used many times. Amalia observed him without making any comment, a kind of smile flickering on her lips like someone who is enjoy-ing a secret theft.

Later they sat and ate. First they ate mamaliga with cheese, and when they finished that, Gad poured warm milk into bowls and in each bowl he put a piece of mamaliga that had hardened.

''Why did you cry when we first came up here?'' Gad sur-prised her.

''I?'' She was about to withdraw a little but recovered im-mediately and said, ''I was afraid.''

''I hate those crowded little villages. They're stifling. Here everything is open and no one tells you what to do.''

''I miss my friend Dunya.''

''Now she's certainly burdened with children and ill-nesses.''

''I could help her.''

''I don't miss a thing. I don't see how it's possible to live together with so many people. Here no one asks you what you've done, where you've gone. Here you don't owe any-one an accounting.''

''But we must visit our parents, mustn't we?''

''And who will stay here?''

Amalia bent her head as though she realized she had said something stupid.

When it got dark she asked for a drink of slivovitz. Gad walked over to the cupboard, and without saying anything he took out the bottle and poured one for her and for himself. He immediately began to talk with a kind of enthusiasm about the marvelous mountaintop, which gave a person what only an isolated place can give. Everyone was in thrall to the well-to-do and the bureaucrats, frittering away their days for nothing. Here was no yoke. Amalia was gripped by his voice, and her eyes never left him. At last he spoke, with the same enthusiasm, about the duty to collect a fixed sum from the pilgrims. Everyone knew there was no such thing as a free guard, so they all had to pay some amount, and if they wished to add something to it, they could. He spoke like the drunken peasants on their way home who resolve that, once they're at home, they'll beat their wives black and blue.

Amalia listened quietly, without comment. Later that night, after she'd drunk quite a few cups and was full of his plentiful, disorganized words, she burst out crying. Gad was surprised by that sudden sobbing. He bent to his knees, and, like the night before, he grasped her foot and sank his mouth in the hollow of her arch. Amalia let out a sharp wail, but she didn't pull her foot away, and, like the night before, he gripped her body and never let it go.

The next day the sky was bright and spotless. The snow was crusted, and on its brilliant surface hopped large crows. Now, with a twinge of his heart, Gad remembered the cemetery and the peaks that surrounded it. For some reason it seemed to him that he had not been there for many days. Fear roused him from his bed, and he rose to his feet.

"What time is it?" asked Amalia.

"It's twelve o'clock."

He rushed to the barn. The neglected, thirsty animal expressed its joy with a few broken moos. When they arrived it had been a young cow that had calved only once, and since then there had been a mute affection between them. It had never kicked him, and he had never struck it. In the mild seasons he took it out to pasture and stayed with it in the open air. During the quiet hours spent at its side, his mind drifted in pleasant daydreams.

Right after milking the cow he said to Amalia, "I'm going up to the cemetery. Give the dogs something to eat."

"Where are you going?" she asked, half asleep.

"To the cemetery."

"Don't walk too far," she said, without opening her eyes.

"I'm here," he said and went out.

The sun was low and radiated light all along the peaks, a bare, cold sun. The visibility was clear and piercing, and below, in the scattered villages, the little cottages stood out bare. The distant, chilled vista reminded him of long winter roads, of his father and the little sled he used to drive. He had gone with him a few times to buy supplies in the villages. Once a snowstorm had trapped them in the fields, and his father, in great despair, had gotten down from the sled and cried out, "Save us, O Lord, save us!" To their surprise the prayer had been answered. The storm stopped swirling, and they reached home.

The cemetery was entirely covered with snow. A few of the taller monuments peeked out above the accumulation. At first he was of a mind to take a shovel and clear it away, but he immediately realized the stupidity of that wish. The snow did no harm. He remembered his Uncle Arieh's words: It was only the melting ice that seeped down and laid bare the tombs. Many months would pass before the spring, and until then there was nothing to do. There was no need to do anything. All at once that thought calmed the fear that had been gnawing at him ever since he opened his eyes.

Over the years he had become attached to the place. More than once he had taken a book of psalms out of his coat pocket and prayed. Here he had seen his father and mother from time to time, people burdened to exhaustion, clutching their small store with their nails, but it was no use. The customers became fewer, the creditors took their bites, and everything collapsed. If there had been any speck of light in that murky space, it was Amalia's glowing face. She was pretty, with a beauty that frightened her parents. More than once he had found his father sitting and staring at her while she slept. Their mother would say one mustn't look at sleeping children, and he stopped, but not completely. He would stare at her in secret. The mother didn't spare her; she used to hit her even after she had grown up into a young woman.

At first it had seemed that no blow would spot that glowing face, but passing time acted otherwise. It secretly furrowed her face, which grew rounder, and above her upper lip the first lines appeared.

When Amalia reached the age of eighteen, a young shopkeeper had wanted to marry her. He was a plump young man who had inherited a large store from his parents and spoke in the decisive fashion of a man who has a great deal of business and no spare time for idle matters. But Amalia, to everyone's surprise, refused. Her mother and aunts remonstrated in vain. She was firm in her resolve: certainly not.

"You'll regret it." Her mother reproached her with gritted teeth. The father did not intervene. Because he did not intervene, she got angry at him too. For weeks the house rumbled like a seething pot. In the end their mother fell ill, with a mortal illness, and never rose from her sickbed. Their father did not live long either. That very winter he fell ill and departed from this world.

Amalia had been eighteen, and Gad was five years older. They tried to save the store, but it was foundering in debt. Finally they had no alternative but to sell. The cash barely sufficed to cover what was owed.

After the days of mourning the house emptied of visitors. Amalia would stand at the window for hours. Her beauty faded. But in Gad's eyes it was unspoiled. He had always loved her timid movements, and the lines hidden in her face. When their Uncle Arieh had invited them up to the mountain peak he had been pleased: From now on he and Amalia would be in the same house.

When he returned to the house, the light in the sky had already dimmed. Amalia was sitting on the floor and playing with the dogs. A strange kind of mirth raced about her eyes.

"What are you doing?" he asked, without looking at her.

"Nothing at all."

"You mustn't let the dogs into the house."

"They were cold."

That old suspicion, that murky suspicion, that she was secretly in love with the dogs lit a dormant flame within him, and again he said, "You mustn't let the dogs into the house." Now it sounded like a reprimand, and she bowed her head.

She hadn't prepared a hot meal again. They ate bread, smoked meat, and sauerkraut. Gad told her how much snow had piled up in the cemetery, and about the sights spread out there. Amalia asked nothing. Only later she surprised him and asked why it was forbidden for Cohens to enter the cemetery. At one time Gad had known all the reasons, but now, somehow, he had forgotten them. Greatly embarrassed he said, "That's what's written. One doesn't ask. One obeys." Amalia smiled. She knew her brother didn't know the reasons.

After the meal they downed a few glasses of slivovitz. Now Gad remembered the Jew who had brought him the bottle, a tall Jew with a proud mien and a thin sort of nobility. His conduct in the cemetery was restrained, but his eyes, large mournful eyes, overflowed with sorrow for which there was no balm.

Later that night, already drunk, Amalia spoke with a mocking fluency about the cold dark days of her childhood, and about her mother, who used to strike her cruelly, and about her father, who was weak and never came to her aid. First Gad tried to console her with words, but when they were of no use, he drew near her and removed her blouse, and with a very powerful movement he hugged and then subdued her.

CHAPTER 13

The following days were cold and dark, and the two stoves couldn't keep the house warm. Amalia sprawled in bed most of the day, only getting up to eat. Gad would prepare full meals, and they sat together at the table. Amalia didn't ask what would happen or how. A kind of thin laughter occasionally burst out from within her and set the silence in the room aquiver. It was difficult to know what was happening inside her. Her face expressed no pain or sadness. Gad spoke a lot about the spring and about his plans to improve the cemetery, so that the place would be accessible and well taken care of. It wasn't just any graveyard, but rather the Cemetery of the Martyrs, who defended the whole Jewish people, he said, like someone who had memorized something. She listened to his recitation without interference. She knew, even in her drunkenness, that nothing would come of his plans. The pilgrims wouldn't respond to his entreaties. They would avoid giving contributions, and without money the peasants wouldn't quarry the stones from the mountain. After sitting for an hour, she would go back and curl up in bed.

"You mustn't sleep so much," he commented, without scolding her.

"I'm tired."

"Prolonged sleep fosters evil thoughts."

"I feel good in bed."

And that was a kind of invitation to come and curl up at her side. Sometimes they didn't get out of bed for a whole day. His thirst for her could not be quenched. Every night he would find new hidden corners in her body. Occasionally a kind of dread would attack him in the middle of the night. He would get up, light the lantern, and go down to the shed to saw firewood. That strenuous labor would blunt the attack, and he would be calmed.

Once, nevertheless, she asked whether it was a sin.

"Certainly," he said, without batting an eyelash.

Upon hearing that answer she spread out both her hands, leaned on the table, raised herself a bit, and said, "I don't care if they punish me." Gad heard her and placed his hands on his cheeks, as though he had been slapped.

One morning a knock was heard at the door, and Amalia got up and slipped down into the cellar. It was an old peasant. Gad was pleased and smiled at him, offering him a drink. The peasant sipped it and told at length of the old days, when he had been young and had come here to sell supplies to Uncle Arieh.

"Why did you come now?" Gad asked impolitely.

The peasant was stunned for a moment, recovered, and said, "I thought you'd buy from me too. Your Uncle Arieh and I were good friends."

"Where will I get money to pay you?" He spoke with him in the old Jewish tone.

"The pilgrims will give to you, and you'll pay me."

"They don't give me a cent."

"I wouldn't let them in. There are no free watchmen in this world."

Gad wanted to make a detailed reply to him, but his supply of words seemed to have given out, and he made a movement with his right hand as if to say, It's too late for me to change. But the peasant didn't give in, and he revealed to him that Uncle Arieh used to demand full payment strenuously, and whoever didn't pay wouldn't get in.

"Uncle Arieh was a believer in the full sense of the word." Gad sought to astonish the peasant. But the peasant wasn't astonished.

He answered simply, "What's the connection between money and faith?"

"I don't know what to do," Gad finally admitted.

"During the summer you must lock the gate, and only those who pay may enter."

"I'll start doing it that way." He gave in.

"And you haven't a penny?" The peasant returned to his business.

"Not a single cent."

"Too bad I dragged myself up here."

"I'd very much like to buy slivovitz from you. I need it like air to breathe. It's our bread and wine." He spoke the peasants' language. "But what can I do? I didn't do my job. I failed."

"What are you saying?"

"Believe me. I'm not exaggerating. There are nights when I see sanctity hovering over this place like a thin cloud. We, to our regret, are unworthy of it. We are impervious to it and impure."

"That's that," said the peasant, rising to his feet.

"I have a valuable ring. If you hadn't known my Uncle Arieh, I wouldn't sell it to you for any price in the world. It's a ring I inherited."

Gad walked to the bureau, untied an old peasant kerchief, and took a ring out of it.

"Gold?" asked the peasant in a peasantlike manner.

"Pure gold."

"And how much do you want for it?"

"Thirty pieces of silver. Not one penny less. If you hadn't known Uncle Arieh, I wouldn't sell it to you. It's a valuable ring, and it would be worth twice as much in the market. Look at it closely and see how much workmanship has been invested in it. It's a nobleman's ring."

"I could do without it gladly. I need cash. No one leaves his home in the winter unless he's in desperate straits."

"That's all I can offer you. It's not easy for me to sell a ring I inherited."

"And how many bottles am I to leave here?"

"Thirty, not one less."

The old man smiled. "Jews are forbidden to drink, isn't that so?"

"In high places like ours it's permitted."

The old man liked the ring, but he didn't show it. He complained about the high price and how hard it would be to sell it. Finally, after bargaining for a long time, he agreed to leave behind twenty bottles of slivovitz, a sack of corn flour, and a wedge of sheep cheese. They sealed the bargain with a handshake, and the peasant spoke once more about Uncle Arieh, not without hidden admiration, because he had been an honest man and a strong one too. The peasants hadn't dared to harm him, and anyone who tried had met with punishment. Gad listened to the peasant's words and felt as though he was being reprimanded.

Gad knew he had done something he shouldn't have. When the time came his flesh would be mortified because of it. Nevertheless his eyes were pleased with the sight of the blue bottles standing on the table.

"Amalia," he called. "The peasant left. I have good news."

Amalia came up from the cellar, and when she saw the bottles on the table, her face glowed, and she said, "A miracle from heaven! Who brought them?"

"A peasant brought them."

"A divine angel."

"You mustn't talk that way."

"But what shall I say?"

"You needn't say anything."

"We were without a drop. What would we have done?"

"We would have overcome."

"I would have gone out of my mind. Without a bottle, life has no purpose."

"You mustn't talk that way."

"But what shall I say?"

"You needn't say anything." He repeated himself, as though that was a general rule appropriate at any time and place.

The winter continued without letup. Gad felt he was cut off from his parents, from his home town, and from the house where he was born. A year ago his mother and father had visited him in his sleep. But they had slowly detached themselves from him. At first he had felt relief, his sleep became transparent and weightless, but in time his slumber had grown muddy, and now he was caught up in it as in a tunnel with no exit.

"Do you still dream?" he would ask.

"I've stopped."

"I've forgotten everyone."

"It just seems that way."

"I feel as though I've never been there."

"That's just momentary."

Amalia had many faces at that time. Sometimes her face

was wrapped in light, as in her childhood, when she used to lean on the windowsill or, on sabbath afternoons, in the neglected hall, a face without blemish. Even then he had feared lest that marvelous face be ruined, and one day her face might look like those of the market women. For a moment he was glad his fear had proven vain, but in the dark, drunken, and confused nights, he saw clearly that no sign of her clear and wonderful face remained. Leathery skin grew on it, which made her jaws prominent, and also her mouth, which was pulled shut most of the day. When the mouth opened a little, bitterness was spread on it. Now, however, the bitterness had faded a little, but in its place grew a kind of hidden hostility, clinging to the folds of skin.

"Amalia." He would call her all of a sudden.

Her gaze, which just a year before had been lively and full of devotion, that marvelous look, was now filled with suspicion. Sometimes it would emerge from her pupils, become sharp, and wound him.

"Why are you angry?" He could no longer restrain himself.

"I'm not angry," she would say and reveal her eyes.

And when she revealed her eyes, he would discover something of her hidden being; she was not the Amalia she had been. There was a kind of bow to her back like the women who had been raped at one time by cossacks. Shame, for some reason, clung to their backs. From a distance one sees that this is Hannah, who was raped. Her son, born to her from the rapist, is banished far away to a crowded town, where they try to remove the flaw from within him.

When he looked at her closely he knew that what he had

done to her that winter would never be erased. She herself did not know into what realms of darkness he had thrown her.

"Forgive me," he would ask her.

"Why?"

"I feel guilty."

"You're mistaken," she would say, with a strange kind of certainty.

Since her childhood he had been attracted by her. True, more than a few times he had found refuge in the bosom of gentile women. He secretly hoped that they, those full and generous women, would root his attraction for her out of his heart, and they, indeed, did what women are meant to do. Yet the attraction did not fade. It seemed to grow stronger with the years and the darkness. Truly it was no longer an attraction but rather a drunken slide. Now he also knew its bottom. If I were a decent and dependable brother I would return her to the Plain, rent her a room, and support her until she finds a decent husband. That's how I ought to have done things, and indeed that's what Uncle Arieh did for his younger sister, he would torment himself. This was merely outward remorse. In fact, now he wanted only to stroke her in that darkness which was growing dimmer day by day.

"Wouldn't you like to go back to the Plain?" He tested her nevertheless.

"I don't want to go anywhere," she would respond, in a voice roughened by alcohol.

"And you aren't frightened?"

"Of what?"

All this was during the daylight hours, but in the after-noon, when the darkness thickened and she had poured a few drinks into herself, she would change, smile, and embrace him shamelessly, as though she had been waiting for that win-ter all those years, for it to enclose them, finally, in that dark shell. After an hour of embraces, she would kneel down and kiss his palms like a person who has lost her entire world and has nothing left but that hand.

That pleasure gradually darkened his spirit. What would happen in the summer, when people came? They would cer-tainly see and know right away. At first she didn't respond to those fears, as if she hadn't absorbed them. Finally she gath-ered strength and said, "No one can take away the little bit that we have."

"I'm frightened."

"Of whom?"

"Of the people who'll be coming in the summer."

"They won't be our judges."

"I know, but they'll spread the rumor."

"I'm not afraid of informers."

Her open, glowing eyes now expressed the freedom of an animal that doesn't know what fear is. Sometimes she would speak fluently and with a kind of wild enthusiasm about the need to be freed from oppressive memories, from dark thoughts, and from fear of people: to live without dread. Her face was not pretty at that time. The dark wrinkles around her eyes would spread out on her temples, and her forehead was narrow and dark. But her voice was clear and strong.

Gad was repelled by the flow and power of her words, and he didn't ask a thing, but when she continued to press him, asking why he was afraid, what difference did it make what people said, he couldn't refrain from saying, "You're right, my dear. I'm wicked, I'm a fool."

CHAPTER 15

The winter grew ever deeper, and every time Gad gathered his strength, wrapped himself in his Uncle Arieh's winter coat, and started to go out and visit the cemetery, a storm would blow up, break out, and block his way. Strong was his will to reach the graves and prostrate himself upon them. He was certain, more than at any other time, that only they had the power to save him. For hours he would stand by the window and wait for a letup.

The cemetery now assumed a new image in his eyes. For some reason it seemed wider to him, as though it had spread out to the vicinity of the abandoned Christian graveyard. He sensed that part of his being, that which was faithful and devoted to Judaism, was buried there and awaiting him. If he managed to join with it, he would be connected not only with himself but also with the entire Jewish people, from whom he had divorced himself.

Amalia did not budge from the stove. On her face a kind of frozen worry solidified ever more. Now it was hard to know what she was thinking. She had indeed been worried, but recently the worry had been buried and forgotten, and now only remnants of it were left.

For many days she waited beside the window. Finally the churning of the storm halted, and broad streaks of blue were revealed in the sky. "I'm going out," said Gad without delay.

"Don't." Amalia tried to stop him, but he did not heed her, and with a lurch, holding a spade in his hand, he went.

He advanced slowly, drawing his feet along cautiously. Then, as though his fears had melted, and with a will such as he had known in his youth, he took powerful, sure steps in the deep snow.

Once again the cemetery was entirely covered with snow, and if his feet had not been familiar with the place, he would not have known it. First he considered clearing away the snow, and indeed he did toss away a few spadefuls, but he immediately grasped the stupidity of his action. For a moment he forgot his purpose in going there. He was seized by the view of the white slopes, which spread out in splendid silence. A few sleds glided along at the foot of the peaks, devouring the distances with ease as though seeking to soar. For a moment Gad saw his father, standing with bent back in the store, illuminated by the light of the snow and with inconsolable sadness on his face. "Father," he called out. Hardly had he uttered the word, before Adiel appeared before his eyes,

the old man who had stood there and preached to those assembled.

As usual, he did not speak about the martyrs but rather
about life, about vain fears, and about those who torture
themselves with futile worries and fail to see the main point
and the purpose. Two men held his arms, but he did not appear to be leaning on them. His voice was clear and strong.
For a moment it seemed he was about to hurl a severe reprimand at the handful of people banded together there. That,
of course, was merely the first impression, and now he came
to the main point of his speech. This is the God of Abraham,
Isaac, and Jacob, and there is no place empty of Him, and, as
it is said, "if I rise up to the heavens, there art Thou, and if I
make my bed in the underworld, Thou art there." True,
greatly reduced and in concealment, but present. Thus one
must never despair but prevail like a lion and draw oneself up
out of the mire. By drawing oneself up, at the same time one
draws up others who are mired in the mud like oneself, and
perhaps from a greater depth.

During the summer the old man's words had sounded distant and as ungraspable as the tractate "Seeds" and other obscure parts of the Mishnah that deal with abstruse and
complex issues. In his heart Gad was incensed at the old man
for not talking in simple language, but now it was as if his
words had become clear, and he understood a bit of them.

It had been a difficult summer. Little rain had fallen, and
choking dryness stood in the air. Processions of peasants
snaked through the valley bearing images and loudly praying
for the end of the drought. Sometimes it had seemed that in a
short while they would climb up on the cliffs and take out

their anger on the handful who had come to prostrate themselves on tombs and beg for mercy. The old man spoke of that as well. He warned them against fears. We must fear only Him who sits on high, for He is a compassionate and merciful God. Fear of death flaws creation. One must accept death quietly, without making a huge commotion.

Meanwhile the sky closed up and heavy snow gripped by the wind broke over the mountaintop. Gad hunched over, but that movement did not help him. The storm knocked him down, and he clung to the surface of the snow and moved on all fours. For a long time he crawled until he reached the foot of the acacia tree. That tall tree, at the foot of which, during the summer, the pilgrims sat, now seemed like a staff planted on the edge of an abyss. He clung to it as to a lifesaving pole. Now he saw death in another guise, not as the old men had described it in their preaching, but rather in the image of a Ruthenian peasant borne on a long pitchfork. "God, take away this monster," he shouted out loud, but he immediately knew his shout would go unanswered, because a person's petition cannot be met while he is unclean.

When, after an hour, at the end of his strength, he reached the doorway, Amalia greeted him with an awkward smile and said, "Where were you?"

"It was hard to get back." He tried to reveal a hand's-breadth of what had happened.

"I was very worried about you, my dear." She was drunk, but her face was pure, as though she had succeeded in shedding the wild skin and in leaving only the little girl within her, and Gad, who wanted to tell her about the terrible things he had encountered on his way, stood mute and did not utter a word.

Finally he said, "Give me a drink." Amalia poured him one without saying anything, and he gulped it down with a single swallow and asked, "Did anyone look for me?"

"No, my dear."

"For some reason it seemed to me that someone was wandering about on the peak and looking for me."

"It just seemed that way."

The last words, which Amalia spoke distractedly and only to calm him, reminded him that he had not done what he intended to do. The part of his soul that was devoted to Judaism had remained there beneath the mounds of ice. That awareness seeped into his limbs with pain, but it did not reach his feet. His feet were frozen.

"What's the matter?" Amalia opened her large eyes.

"The storm attacked me." He no longer hid the truth.

"You mustn't go out in such weather."

"What could I do?"

Amalia, who knew his soul, stepped over to the sink to prepare hot soup for him, a cheese pie, and some pickled cucumber. Gad sat at the table and silently devoured everything his sister served. She sat not far from him and looked at his face. His face was dark like that of a man who has seen dreadful sights.

After he had eaten the meal she drew close, leaned over, removed his soaking shoes, and wordlessly began to rub his frozen toes.

Many thoughts raced about his brain, but one gradually become ensconced in it, and this is what it was: As soon as the snow melted, he would take the small box, put in the jewels that had been left to them by Uncle Arieh, the money, and the two gold watches, and give them to Amalia, rent a wagon, and send her back to their native town.

The storms stopped, and a quiet frost, a burning frost, crouched in the cracks of the windows. Amalia brought Mauzy and Limzy into the house, and Gad made no comment. He spent most of the hours of the day in the shed sawing wood, and when he came in from there his face was dark like that of a man gripped by harsh dreads.

Amalia sensed that evil thoughts haunted him, and she toiled. What she had not done all winter, she did now. She prepared cheeses and butter, she baked and did laundry, and at noon the meal would be ready on the table. Sometimes he would rouse from his gloom and ask, "Has anyone been here?"

"No."

"It seemed to me that someone was walking around."

"All the paths are blocked," she said. Now she was the practical one, listening to the outdoors, taking care of the dogs, rising early to milk the cow. Gad would stand for hours by the window, make reckonings, and mutter. Once, distractedly, he said to Amalia, "I'm sorry I gave the ring to that peasant. Who knows what harm I did."

"We had nothing to drink." She tried to mollify him.

"We mustn't drink," he burst out. A new gloom covered his face. Amalia did not respond to those outbursts. She would serve him a drink as though offering medicine to a patient. A kind of spryness took over her, as during the months when their father had lain sick and she had tried to save him with hot water bottles, thin porridge, and a great deal of devotion, but nothing had worked, and he had been snatched away all at once.

That devotion inspired him, creating words that he had not dared to utter previously, and their main point was: "You must return home. You mustn't be away from home for so much time. Here everything is dangerous. Only at home, only among Jews, is one protected."

"What will I do alone down below?" She tried to arouse his mercy.

"We have cousins."

"I've already become accustomed to the mountain peak."

"You mustn't be here."

And when he would press her with his words, she would say, "And what about you?"

"I'll be here. The devil won't take me away."

"Alone?"

"Nothing will happen to me."

Once she tried a different tack. "But we've sold the house."

"I'll give you the inheritance. You can rent a house. You can live decently."

"I don't need a house."

"What do you want?"

Now the long nights came, cold and muted, nights during which almost nothing was said. Amalia would serve him a plate of soup and bread, without asking anything or requesting anything. She would eat her meals next to the stove. Nor did Mauzy and Limzy whimper, as if they knew their presence in the house was by special grace.

When he finally took out the box and placed it on the bench, she could no longer restrain herself, and she said, "If that is what you wish, I shall respect it."

"If I could, I would go down with you. But I swore to guard this holding."

"I understand," she said, not showing she felt scorned.

"A person must return home, isn't that true?"

"Correct." She interrupted him.

"What can I do?"

She bowed her head as though it were not her loving brother speaking to her but rather a cunning, violent peasant. Now she realized: a few thick lines had grown on his face,

Unto the Soul · 89

giving it a coarse expression. Soldiers would return with faces like that after serving long sentences in military prisons.

Now she no longer pleaded. Her face closed up, and something of their sick mother's pride showed at her temples. The winter continued without letup, and the darkness was full and opaque. Gad would have a few drinks, and the thick lines on his face would fill with a muddy redness. Strangely, that ugliness did not pain her. What pained her were his groveling, the contradictions, and the lies.

Sometimes he would apologize and say, "It's not my fault, it's the way of the world. We aren't free in this world. In the summer people will come and discover it immediately. Things like these are impossible to hide." Thus he would sit and heap up words, each word paining her, but she made no comment to him, though once she did say, "Other people are apparently important to you, because you live by their dictate." Gad heard her and restrained himself. Later, without warning, he opened up the caged shed and sent the dogs out with kicks.

Sometimes, in order to appease her, he said, "What do you suggest?"

"Nothing."

"But you're angry with me."

"I'm not angry."

She would get up while it was still dark and begin working immediately. In her heart she was sorry for her big brother, her brother whom she had loved since childhood, who was afraid now of what people would say. She wanted to shout: We mustn't be afraid of people; even if a person commits serious sins, he mustn't be afraid of people. We are delivered over only to God. He is the Father, and He is the Judge, not people. People are evil and hypocritical. They have no innocence. That is what she wanted to shout.

For hours she would sit and look at him. It angered her that her beloved brother's walking was stooped and gloomy, his spirit cloudy, and that toward evening he would sit in the corner like a persecuted man.

CHAPTER 17

While the house was still full of darkness, Gad was sawing wood without pause. Amalia was sorting potatoes in the cellar, and odors of rot mingled with the smell of sauerkraut wafted through the house. Everything stood as though it were about to be frozen, then a south wind broke out and drove away the clouds, all at once laying bare a huge sun, a round sun, and the spaces all around, which for months had lain contracted in gloom, were opened, raised up, and filled with brightness. Gad went out the door and stepped back immediately, but Amalia put out her hand and proclaimed, like a child, "Sun in the sky, sun."

"This joy is premature." Gad spoke doubtfully. His way of sitting curled up next to the window said, One mustn't rejoice, one mustn't trust, one must fear the morrow, which will be harder than anything we have known. Afterward too, when he went outside, the milk pail in his hand, he looked like a destitute village beggar, short and full of trepidation. No trace remained of his erect stature.

The frost was still bitter, but it was a different kind of cold, a sunny cold, that reminded one of youth and the will to live. Amalia went out and fed the dogs. The dogs, who had grown thick fur, were happy and expressed their joy with merry leaps. Amalia let them off their chains and said, ''Go forth into the wide open spaces, go forth into freedom.'' At the same time Gad headed mechanically for the woodshed. Before long the dull and rhythmical sound of sawing was heard throughout the house. For a moment she wanted to go down to the woodshed and beg him, tell him, I can't stand that sawing. My head is splitting. The sun has returned to us, and we don't need any more firewood. Later she went down and for the first time she saw her brother at work. He looked like a convict sentenced to forced labor who had been given an impossible task, and he was struggling with all his might to do it, frightened that a guard would come in the evening and beat him mercilessly. Now she saw him at work, she didn't dare open her mouth.

The next day the sky was clear and spotless, and immediately after the milking Gad went out to the cemetery. He took short, slow steps, like someone who expects no salvation from anyplace else. Now Amalia remembered her brother who just a few years ago had been full of faith, innocence, and the will to act. Punctual about the times for prayer, on sabbath afternoons he would read through the weekly Torah portion. Only during the third year of their presence there had the strangeness spread out within him. He had grown stout, and his gait had become cautious and heavy. First that had seemed like a trivial change, but in time it became clear that the place was kneading him in its mighty hand, giving him the look of a Ruthenian peasant. Earlier he had been angry with Amalia for not lighting the sabbath candles, but soon he had stopped that. The days became mingled with one another, and time stretched out in an unbroken flow into the dark abyss.

In the evening Gad returned to the house, and a cloud surrounded his face. He sat at the table and did not utter a word.

"How are things up on the top?" Amalia asked cautiously.

"The frost hasn't thawed yet."

"I intend to clean out the synagogue."

"It's too early."

"I want to clean everything before I leave."

"For where?"

"Home."

He knew this was the critical moment. "I won't send you down below unless it's your wish."

"I'll arrange everything and come back," she replied quietly.

Hearing that answer, it was as if the dam of his heart had burst, and he spoke about this cold and cursed place that eats up a man's marrow, also saying that the people who came here were not all decent. If they had stayed down below, they now would have a shop and a faithful clientele. Amalia did not reply to his words. She walked over to the stove and, with quick movements, prepared his supper. Before long Gad sank into the bowl of soup, as though there were nothing in his world except that hot liquid.

When he finished the soup he remembered that the day before he had dreamed about the house, their mother, and the store. Their mother was standing by the scale, weighing flour. Suddenly she lifted her eyes and said, "What have you done to Amalia?" Her look was bad and cruel, as when she used to beat Amalia. "Now she cannot be helped in this world."

"It wasn't I." He tried to slip away.

"It was you." She said, without holding onto him.

She immediately returned to the scale and her customers. Gad wanted to beg for his soul, but his mouth was as though filled with gravel. When he woke up the dream was buried. All that day a heaviness oppressed his heart, and only now did the murky dream rise up and flood him again.

"It doesn't matter what people say. It isn't their concern," he said. It was evident that that sentence had occupied him for hours.

"I feel I must go down below."

The words "I feel" startled him up from his seat, and he said, "If that is your wish, I shall not stand in your way."

"I want to clean the synagogue."

"There's no need. All the holy places are neglected."

"It isn't proper."

"Anyway, no one contributes. That's what they deserve, no more." Gad remembered that sentence, which he had once used often.

"I must do it."

"Do what you want. I won't mix in," he said and stepped aside. It seemed to Amalia that he was about to go down to the shed to do his daily task, to the saw and the stumps of wood.

Amalia worked from morning to late at night. Gad helped her, but not willingly. He spent most of the day in the cemetery. The snow was melting, and he would stand for hours and wait for the earth to show. The thin bubbling and the muffled fall of clumps of snow reminded him of the sights of former days. Where, he did not remember. A prolonged absence from the cemetery uprooted his memories of the past as well.

The sun swept down from its path and performed simple miracles. It melted layer after layer, and before many days had passed the high plain was fully revealed to the eye. The peaks spread out white and soft, and azure geese, fleeing from their cages, flew about in the sky and voiced wild screeches. In the distance the great river overflowed its banks, the Prut, and its mighty flow could be heard even up here.

In the evening he told Amalia about the miracles that had met him during the day. How layer after layer had melted and the holy gravestones were revealed to the eye. Amalia listened with great tension. She was glad that his hidden feelings had taken form and he was speaking of them with familiar words. He spoke for a long time, as though it were not just a quiet thaw but subtle revelations of colors and sounds. She thought of announcing to him that she was about to go down soon, but seeing his joy she did not dare to put an end to it. She served him a hot meal and sat at his side.

The next day too he returned joyfully. Great words had returned to him, and he used them as before, without restraint. Now Amalia knew that, unlike her, he was attached to the holy graves and drew his vitality from them. Now he no longer spoke of the people's miserliness, their blindness and selfishness, but rather of clear visions and the subtle bonds that sustain the soul. His eyes glowed as after taking a few drinks during the winter, but now the muteness had been shattered, and the words streamed out from him with enthusiasm.

And what will become of me? What will happen if it turns out that I'm pregnant? Her fears awoke within her all at once. Up to now she had not dared think about that. Gad's enthusiasm and the high words he had spoken to her drew up her dread as though from a dark pit: What will be? The hope that in a few days she would return to her native town and all the sins of the winter would be forgotten and plunged into oblivion—that hope, which offered the promise of a way out, was abruptly ended. Gad was immersed within his small joy, and he did not notice that her world had been destroyed all at once. He kept on in his own way with a kind of swelling exhilaration, and as he continued, his face threw off its old dark skin, and oranges and pinks blossomed on his forehead.

In the evening his mood fell off. The great words that had fluttered like banners on his lips fell silent, and he sat, withdrawn, next to the window as though he has been emptied of all will. Nor did the cloud pass from his face next day. He sat in the corner and watched her movements in the house. Finally he said, "What is all that cleanliness for? Why all that polishing? Only ritual bathhouses give off that smell of lye all the time." Amalia didn't understand what he said. It seemed to her that the notion of her pregnancy had also reached him. You have nothing to fear; I'm taking all the responsibility upon myself, she wanted to assure him. His depression brought him near to her, and she sensed that a hint of her soul, which had been hidden within him, was returning to her. In the long dark winter nights they had not spoken much, but his sensations had streamed over to her and filled her. Now she felt that the warm closeness of the dark winter nights, that blazing closeness which she had tried to drive out of her memory, had, as it were, been aroused and rekindled. Suddenly it seemed to her that those bare days were nothing but a trick of the light, and in a short while the dark clouds of winter would return, the frost and the winds, and they would burrow again into the thick pillows as in the blind and happy days.

"The weather isn't stable. I wouldn't be surprised if it

rained tomorrow," she said distractedly. Hearing those words, Gad raised his eyes and his clouded look confirmed that he too expected it.

The twilight dwindled over a long while, and Gad fell asleep in his clothes on the couch. First she wanted to wake him, but when she saw his position, a shrunken, folded position, she sensed it would be better to leave him. His heavy boots, soiled with mud, expressed what his face had not been able to show: the descent into oblivion.

At night she decided within herself that if the sunny days persisted and the snow melted, it was a sign that she must leave the place, but she would not return to her native town and to disgrace; rather, she would travel to one of the old Christian women in Moldovitsa. Women went to those crones to give birth in secret. Afterward they left the babies on the convent steps, and the nuns took them in and raised them. If they were good, they trained them for religious vows. That thought, which had occurred to her by chance, pleased her, as though she had found an escape hatch from the dark tunnel, but when she closed her eyes and fell asleep, broad spaces were spread before her, yellow expanses after the harvest. She was alone, as though she had been thrown out of a wagon loaded with people, and it was clear no one would come and redeem her from that desert place. Henceforth only the low skies, cold skies, would protect her.

CHAPTER 19

What he had feared happened: the spring, in its full light, appeared. The hidden hope of an endless winter, which he had secretly harbored, seemed to slap him on the face. The sky grew higher, bluer, and Gad now knew that Passover, the holiday he loved best of all, had already been celebrated down below, and it could be that also the Feast of Weeks was behind them. As for him and Amalia, it was as though the darkness had thrown them up on the shores of another continent, an illuminated continent where everything was exposed and there was no place to hide.

Amalia stood at the door of the synagogue with her sleeves rolled up, the bucket in her right hand, like someone caught out of place. Why don't you hide? Don't you see that everything lies open to danger? He wanted to call out. Amalia didn't move. The bright sights all around imprisoned her, and she stood enchanted.

"Amalia," he called out.

"What?"

"What are you going to do?"

"I want to clean out the sanctuary."

"There's no need. Holy places ought to be neglected."

Upon hearing that answer she smiled, and the bright ruddiness of her childhood days once again blossomed on her cheeks.

"There's no need," he called out again. "Now we have to see what the snows have done." He spoke loudly, as though to a deaf woman.

"I'm going to go away soon. I wouldn't want to leave dirt behind," she answered, also in a loud voice.

"Where are you going?" he asked in the old domestic way.

"Home," she answered weakly.

"Not now," he said and looked to the side.

Amalia was about to answer him with a long sentence, but he moved away abruptly. His departure was so sharp and hasty that she did not manage to utter a word.

Without turning his head, he strode toward the cemetery. The melting snow had swept a little earth into the drainage ditches, but there hadn't been much erosion. Little puddles glistened in these ditches, and Gad was pleased that the damage was not great; in a day or two the water would seep away and the earth would dry.

It was only when he stood in the clearing that he grasped

how long the winter had been and how the darkness had kept
him from keeping track of time. The remorse that had
seethed within him like venom for many days, remorse he
had not heeded, rose up and emerged from its hiding place. It
seemed to him that a year ago at this season he had already
weeded the orchard and prepared the vegetable beds, but
now everything still was untamed. Amalia, he was about to
call out, we have been lazy all this time. We shall be held ac-
countable for this laziness. No sin goes without punishment
in this world. The words rolled about in his head for a moment and then floated off.

A year earlier an old man with a noble face had stood in the
clearing and asked protection from the martyrs. A typhus epidemic was raging in the region, and it had struck down many
victims. For two days the old man had stood there, fasting. ''I
shall not move from here until they receive their due from
heaven.'' Thus he proclaimed whenever people approached
him and asked him at least to sit down. Calm was in his face.
After two days of standing in one place, the silent stance of a
soldier on guard, he took several steps backward, bowed, approached the bench, and sat down. Others sprawled on the
stones, wept, and counted their sins like bargaining peddlers.
There was no lack of confidence men who brought dubious
merchandise to the mountaintop to sell it to the gullible. And
there was someone who wrote down the names of all the
saints on a pink tablet and offered it for the price of a piece of
silver. He claimed the names were a charm against all
plagues, that even lepers had been saved.

Later, when Gad returned to the synagogue, he found it
silent and washed. The smell of fresh lye wafted through the

air. The light and the moisture gave the place a new simplicity. He nearly went to the bookshelf to take out a prayerbook. During the first year he had prayed regularly. During the second year he had come to pray occasionally. But since then, contact with the books had become more difficult every year. When the people come, I'll pray; he acknowledged his duty. But it was precisely the recollection of the pilgrims that brought the odor of winter darkness to his nostrils, the roaring stove and Amalia's rumpled face. "You should go back home," he called out, "soon."

The daytime hours passed, and he did nothing. Thoughts carried him from place to place, and when he returned to the house, he found it wide open and flooded with light. Amalia stood in the courtyard and groomed the brown cow with a large brush. The wet animal submitted.

"Lord Almighty, what are you doing?" He raised his voice.

Amalia was startled by his sudden shout and said, "Did I make a mistake?"

"There are more pressing things." He interrupted her.

"I'm ready to do anything," she said, without releasing the bucket from her hand.

"The cow can wait. Nothing will happen to it."

"The cow was very dirty."

"It can wait."

"I'll step aside. I won't do anything. If what I do isn't wanted, I won't do a thing," she said and put the bucket aside. Those words, seeking to express abnegation and willingness to obey, kindled Gad's rage, and he spoke with increasing anger about that holy place which had been entrusted to him, so there would be a window to heaven, and now it was a neglected field; not even a single path was cared for.

For a long while he stood in the courtyard and spoke aloud of the need to raise up the ruins of the winter, and first of all to uproot the weeds while they were only sprouting, for if they didn't pull them out now, they would spread and cover the entire place, and it would be impossible to overcome the neglect. This was not her beloved brother but another man who was rolling strange and hostile words about in his mouth. Amalia stood frozen and silent. Her silence kindled his rage even more, and he turned to her with a theatrical gesture and said, "Go. You don't care. You want to go down and leave everything on my shoulders. I cannot bear that burden."

Amalia burst out crying, and Gad approached her.

"Weeping won't change the facts." He pronounced a sentence to her that he had heard years earlier in the market.

"You torture me from morning to night." The words were strangled in her mouth.

"I don't do anything to you. I want to open up your eyes."

"I cleaned everything and washed everything."

"That's not important."

"What is important? Tell me so I'll know."

"We have to pull out the weeds, to pluck them out while they're just sprouting, otherwise they'll spread, and it will be impossible to pull them out anymore." A sharpness was in his voice, the sharpness of a bark.

"Don't hit me so hard," she said and retreated into the house.

"I don't hit."

"Every night you beat me like a beast of the field. If you don't want me, send me away, but don't strike me."

"I don't hit."

"You hit me with the ox goad. My whole body is a wound and a bruise. I can't bear it any longer."

It was hard for him to fall asleep that night. The weeping and the mumbling, "Don't hit me, Don't hit me," seeped into his ears. He was angry that his beloved sister was making false accusations. The matter of the trip home now seemed to him like a kind of unfair evasion. He forgot, of course, that he himself had raised the idea.

Later he remembered that Amalia had not said, Don't hit me with the whip but with the ox goad, which showed she couldn't have meant it seriously. That thought rolled about in his tired brain and consoled him for a moment, and he fell asleep.

CHAPTER 20

Afterward the spring showed its marvels, and Gad sank into his work. The bushes all around blossomed, and the dark peaks were covered with a green carpet. The visibility was clear, and it was possible to see the distant villages distinctly, spread out at the foot of the mountains. Horses drew long wagons, laden with clover, and they, for some reason, reminded him of expansive life throbbing to the pulse of the seasons, without anger and without pain.

They did not discuss the matter of the trip. One evening when she asked, "When will I go home?" he answered impatiently. "There's time. Not now." Her face grew rounder, and health throve in her limbs. The fetus in her womb throbbed, and she could feel it every hour of the day.

What would happen and how her life would be managed from now on, she did not know. In nightmares she would see the path homeward, and she was rolling down it and fall-ing into the heart of the fish market. Robust women stood next to the broad stalls, and red fish flopped in their hands. When she awakened she knew clearly that she would not re-turn there. The old gentile women in Moldovitsa are better for me.

Gad too nurtured hope in his heart. Perhaps a miracle would happen for him, and people wouldn't come this time. Four years earlier the summer had been pleasant and green, and Gad had expected a lot of people, but robbers cast their dread upon the roads, and only a few reached the peak, frightened people who prayed in haste and returned whence they had come. He hardly exchanged a word with Amalia. She worked with severe diligence from morning on, and in the evening, upon returning from the vegetable garden, she would prepare a hot meal. Sometimes, overtired, she would fall asleep without tasting anything.

"Why don't we have a drink?" He would turn to her from time to time, seeking closeness. She would respond and drink two or three glasses. But no conversation emerged from those sips. Even practical words were scarce in her mouth. From time to time she would nevertheless utter two or three words, which she had used in her childhood. The words would brighten his face all at once. But the fears were hardest of all, they silently bubbled up and poisoned even the clear twilight that softly seeped through the windows.

"Amalia." He would suddenly address her.

"What?"

With those words a whole night would sometimes be ex-hausted.

One evening Gad returned from the cemetery, his face ruddy from the sun, and a strange force abounded in his shoulders and neck. Amalia recoiled. That evening her brother seemed like one of the Ruthenian peasants who, during their holidays, would terrify the Jewish market stalls; there was always someone killed or several people wounded. Their father too, that gentle and beloved soul, had not escaped from them unscathed. On one of their holidays, a peasant had brought a sledgehammer down upon him. Amalia was then five years old, and the sight of that brawny peasant was engraved in her eyes. Her father had suffered for years from the injured shoulder, but he did not complain, as though it were his private secret.

"You must return home," said Gad, when he had consumed his meal.

"I'm ready," she answered immediately.

"I see no other possibility if we are not to commit suicide."

"We could repent," she said, as though he had threatened her with a drawn knife.

"For some deeds there can be no repentance." He continued striking.

"I will try to do everything in my power," she said. She was no longer defending herself but the embryo in her womb.

Gad bent his head, and it was evident that the words he had spoken had been simmering for many days, and now that he had brought them up from the hollows they had weakened him, as it were.

"Soon wagons will come, and I'll descend." She spoke, not in her own voice.

Her acquiescence apparently frightened him. He let Mauzy and Limzy off their chains and went out to take what he had once called "a turn with the dogs." That sudden departure seemed to her like a new threat, and she stood frozen next to the window. Meanwhile she remembered that once on Yom Kippur eve one of the old men had stood and preached about the scapegoat upon which all the sins of the Jews were hung, and how they plunged over a cliff into the abyss. Then it had sounded distant and frightening, like the ash of the red heifer and the bitter cursed waters, but now it sounded like a clear threat: the slope. When he returned to the house, his face, to her surprise, was quiet, and he spoke about the vegetable gardens and the orchard. Everything was plentiful. Even if the people didn't come, there would be enough to eat, he concluded with strange practicality.

Later, as though remembering, he spoke with great excitement about the peak. Regrettably, angry people shattered its silence. The place must be silent. It was forbidden to arouse it from its silence. He spoke in a calm voice, and something of the light returned to his face.

Amalia said, "We shall always remember the peak."

"Why do you say 'shall remember'?" he scolded her.

"I was mistaken."

"You mustn't be mistaken. We have a great obligation."

That evening Amalia knew this was no longer her brother of bygone days. His face was open, he was not angry, and he did not raise his voice. His gait was quiet and measured. Also, the words he spoke to her were familiar, but the tone was frightening. When he said "I want" or "I am going," it was as though he were not speaking about his own will or about his own motion. Also, his drinking was not like in the past. He would pour down a drink with a narrowing of his eyes and bite his lips. When Amalia asked whether to serve him more soup, he would say, "No need. That was more than enough." In his day their father used to say "more than enough," but since his death no one had used that phrase. Now she was afraid not of her brother's anger but of the silence that hung on his face like a mask, and when he returned to the house in the evening he would sometimes fall asleep on the couch without tasting anything.

While they were still secretly looking forward to reasons that might prevent people from coming, Mauzy broke away from his chain and ran away. At first it seemed like an outburst of joy. He quickly climbed up the slope, and when he reached the end he began to bark. There was no sign of anything bad in that barking. Gad stood in the courtyard and called to him: "Mauzy, come home, don't go wild." Upon hearing Gad's familiar call, he did indeed come down and approach the courtyard. Now it seemed he was about to return to his chain. Amalia bent to her knees, planning to welcome him back with petting. But precisely that gesture drove him out of his mind, and he reared up and bared his fangs as though he intended to pounce. Gad was quicker and hit him. The dog went wild. First it stayed in one place, then it raced out to circle around the peak. It came back and rushed at them. Having no choice, they retreated to the house. "Limzy, why don't you come out and help your brother?"

Amalia called out in desperation. Mauzy circled the peak in a mad run and returned to storm the door. Gad, without asking Amalia's opinion, went down into the cellar, opened up the hiding place, and removed the shotgun from its bed of straw. He stood at the window and aimed the barrels. The shot thundered, and the pellets killed the dog on the spot.

That night they sat next to the open windows and gulped down drink after drink. Gad spoke about Mauzy's wickedness and about his earlier sins. Several times he had attacked pilgrims, and once he had even bitten an old Jew. It seemed to Amalia, for some reason, that he was not speaking about Mauzy but about things that had happened to him in his distant childhood, about oppressive burdens that the years had not wiped away, which floated up whenever a crack was opened. That, of course, was an error in hearing. Gad stood and listed Mauzy's sins one after the other, like a peddler. Finally he summed them up categorically: he had not died by chance. A can of worms had been lying on his back.

When she grasped, finally, that he was talking about Mauzy's old offenses, she became angry at Gad for speaking about Mauzy without mercy. If there had been moments of pleasant tranquility on this dark peak, they were moments passed in the company of Mauzy and Limzy. True, Gad sometimes used to be incensed at their closeness, but he himself liked to walk around the peak with them, and more than once she had found them curled up together on the floor.

Now Mauzy was lying dead in a ditch. The thought of big Mauzy, who had grown thick fur during the winter, who liked to doze off on the floor in a heedless sprawl, responding to being patted and yawning with pleasure—the thought that that friendly creature had become a ferocious animal all at once filled her body with dread, and she was seized with trembling.

"What happened to poor Mauzy?" She tried to defend him for a moment.

"He went out of his mind," he answered, almost offhandedly. Hardly had the words left his mouth when he remembered that Uncle Arieh had told him a few days before his death that the peasants had once tried to poison Mauzy and Limzy, but he had discovered them in time and run after them and caught them. They admitted it and swore they wouldn't do it again. He had let them go on their way.

"The peasants are always trying to poison our dogs." He spoke distractedly.

"Why do they do that? What harm did those creatures do them?"

"It's very simple: to make it easier for them to steal."

Hearing that practical answer, her voice trembled, and she said agitatedly, "He died innocent."

Gad, for some reason, was wounded by her words and said, "No one kills a dog because he's a dog."

"But they poisoned him." The old tone returned to her voice.

"Right. What could we have done? You saw with your own eyes how dangerous he was."

"Wasn't it possible to save him?"

"A poisoned dog is as good as dead." He was glad to have found the correct words.

Amalia bent her head. All her fears were enfolded in her face. That is how she sat after her father died. For a moment he was about to stand up and scold her, but his words were mute and he withdrew. After a long silence, he said, "We mustn't wallow in the memory of animals. Trees too collapse."

"How can we forget them?" she asked, with the wonderment of a child.

"We must forget them. We must even forget our own dead. This world and the next world are not connected to each other." He remembered the voice of one of the old men.

"Mauzy loved us." She spoke with a choked voice.

"As long as he was sane," he said, feeling that words were returning to him.

"We didn't kill him."

"You're right. We watched over him. But the peasants conspired against him. We only saved him from tortures."

Upon hearing those words, tears welled in her eyes. She restrained herself and didn't cry.

Later Gad tried to distract her. He spoke about the fence he had restored without the help of gentiles, and how he would put up a fine gate. The old gate had rotted out over the many years. Once again he was her familiar brother, whose big eyes often reflected a childish innocence, and now when he again spoke about the fence and about the gate, it was as though that innocence had returned and grown stronger in his eyes.

"Too bad we don't know how to pray." She surprised him.

"True," said Gad, as though he had been shown to be in the wrong.

"When I was a little girl I knew how to pray."

"Sometimes I have a strong desire to pray." He clutched at her voice.

"Why have we lost prayer?" The wonderment lit up in her eyes.

"I hope it will come back to us one day. The pilgrims sometimes give me back the desire to pray. You have to learn to pray for the whole community, and then you are answered. Whoever prays for the whole community is answered first," he said and smiled.

"What happened?" Amalia was alarmed by his smile.

"I have lost the feeling for the whole community." The laughter froze on his face.

"Once Father told me one doesn't ask questions, one opens the prayerbook and prays."

"He was right. When one does the right thing for the wrong reason, it's still the right thing," he said, laughing again for using words that were not his own.

"When I open a prayerbook, I choke immediately."

"One starts to pray and overcomes that." The former voice returned to him, the voice of the older brother.

"We are living in sin, aren't we?" She chuckled and hid her face in her right hand.

"We haven't harmed anyone." Gad rose from his seat. "We are guarding this place faithfully. The summer comes to us very late, and we don't always have vegetables."

"True." She tried to join with his voice.

"Everyone who lives down in the Plain ought to know that our task is not an easy one here."

"I must return to the Plain."

"Not now. You'll go down when the time comes. But not now." He repeated those words with a strange kind of emphasis. That night they consumed two bottles, but they weren't drunk. Gad would say over and over, "Our task is not easy, but we shall do what is incumbent upon us." Amalia's face grew rounder, and the wonderment did not leave it. Suddenly she raised her head as if about to tell him, You say the same sentence over and over. Gad grasped her mute comment, but he did not have the power to be still.

Later the acknowledgment of Mauzy's death filled her body, and she said out loud, "Mauzy is no longer among the living. It's hard to understand that. We will miss him a lot. Mauzy, may he rest in peace."

Gad roused from his fatigue and said, "You don't say 'May he rest in peace' about a dog."

"What do you say?"

"You don't say anything."

"He lived with us for seven years in a row."

"What do you want from me?" he said, and his body sank onto the couch.

Next day they slept late, and when they woke up the sun stood high in the sky and it was ten o'clock. "All night I dreamt about our town," said Amalia, without moving from her bed.

"And what did the dreams show you?"

"The town was quiet, but no one remembered me. I remembered everyone, but they didn't remember me."

"And you didn't remind them?" He intervened.

"I didn't know what to say, as though they hadn't ever seen me. I wasn't afraid, but I had a feeling of heaviness. It was hard for me to walk. It was summer, like here, but still it was very hard for me to walk."

"And you didn't say, 'I'm Amalia'?"

"It didn't occur to me."

"What did you do?"

"I went down the narrow street to the Ruthenian market. There they remembered me and asked about you. I told them I was pregnant."

"What did they say?"

"Nothing. They were glad to see me and handed me pears."

Gad went outside. Limzy greeted him with barks of joy, and he gave the dog leftovers from the night, sausage and spinach pie. The courtyard was open and lit up, and from the shaded corners arose the odor of damp plants. Mauzy's death didn't show on Limzy. He ate with a good appetite, seemingly happy not to compete for food. The sky was high and pure, and a sharp silence was spread over the peaks. Not until he opened the barn did Gad remember and know that dreams had tortured him all night too.

In the empty women's section of the synagogue had sat the old teacher Reb Hayim Yosef, who examined him on the subject of the ash of the red heifer. When he was a boy he had known that chapter perfectly, but now it was virtually erased from his head. His prolonged silence aroused the old man from his fatigue, and he asked, "Don't you remember anything? Not even a single detail?"

"No, sir, Rabbi."

"Why are you calling me 'sir' and 'Rabbi'?" The old man opened his eyes wide.

"Isn't that what you're supposed to be called?"

"I'm not a sir and I'm not a rabbi." The old man raised his voice.

"Pardon me."

"When you were six years old you were tested, and you knew it, and now you don't know a thing."

"What can I do?"

"If that's how things are," said the old man, "I can close my eyes. There's no good in examining your deeds. Without memory a man is comparable to an animal, and an animal is judged neither leniently nor harshly. Do you understand?" He closed his eyes.

When Gad returned from the barn, Amalia was still lying curled up in bed.

"Didn't you make a cup of coffee?" he asked in a crushed voice.

"Right away," she said and jumped out of bed.

Amalia poured a little kerosene on the chopped wood and lit the stove. She took butter and cheese out of the pantry and placed them on the table. Light filled the kitchen and the two bedrooms.

"Did something happen?" Amalia asked.

"Nothing. I'm hungry."

Amalia sliced the bread, put down two plates, and touched the kettle with her fingers. "In a little while," she said in her normal voice.

Nevertheless, he couldn't restrain himself. "Couldn't you have lit the stove and made me a cup of coffee?"

Amalia did not reply. She bent her head, and the brightness from the window illuminated her.

After the meal Gad took the spade and the hoe and headed toward the peak near the house. Amalia did not ask him where he was going. She followed his movements closely as he departed until he was out of sight. Apparently his senses had betrayed him. Mauzy had not fallen immediately. He had kept running. Gad found him with his mouth wide open, sprawled in a ditch. An expression of anger had congealed on his face. Dogs always leave the world with an expression of anger. The thought flashed through his mind.

He immediately set to work. He dug a long deep trench, and without hesitation he walked over to the carcass and picked it up with his two hands, immediately laying it in the trench. That work, which didn't take a long time, left his arms very weak, but he recovered himself, took up the hoe, and within a few minutes filled the pit.

Afterward, as though distracted, he loaded the spade and the hoe on his shoulder and turned in the direction of the cemetery. For a long time he walked without any thoughts. The morning lights were warm, and they filtered through his shirt. That contact evoked a desire to lay his body on the earth, to close his eyes and be absorbed into the pleasant silence for a while. But he immediately grasped that first he must return home and wash his fouled hands.

When he got back to the house, Amalia was standing by the window. After he left the house she had stood up to watch him. In her imagination she had seen Mauzy, not shot and dead but sunk in a deep slumber. That impression had grown stronger within her when she saw how he had picked up the carcass with his two hands and placed it in the trench. But when he had taken the hoe in his hands and started to heap clods of earth into the trench, she knew the truth and called out loud, "Don't hurt him, don't hurt him," and she immediately froze in place. Thus she stood by the window until Gad entered the house.

"He apparently died without pain." He tried to sweeten her sadness a little. That consideration raised a twisted smile on Amalia's lips, and she hid her face in both hands. Now it seemed to him that she was about to burst into tears, so he addressed her clearly, saying, "You mustn't weep over animals. Even over humans you mustn't cry too much." Hearing that reprimand, she took her hands away from her face and the twisted smile slipped on her lips. Gad added, "The Sages warned us not to become too attached to animals. They corrupt the spirit."

Afterward he approached the water barrel and washed his hands with lye soap. The angry expression of the dog once again appeared before his eyes. The desire to bite had not ceased with his death. It's good that he departed the world, Gad thought.

Amalia asked, in a voice not her own, "Are you going to the cemetery?"

"I have to finish the fence and prepare the gate. The pilgrims are about to show up."

"We're going to have cucumbers in the garden again," she replied irrelevantly.

"We have to guard the vegetable gardens and the orchard. That's a secure living. Who knows who will come and what they'll bring?"

At first he was going to take the spade with him, but he remembered that the spade was impure and he had to plunge it into the earth to purify it, which is what he did.

On the way he remembered that Passover and the Feast of
Weeks had been lost in time, and there was no sign within
him that they had come. A sort of belated remorse pinched
his chest. In the first year of their sojourn on the mountaintop
they had still held a Passover Seder. Amalia had made the
stove and their utensils fit for the holiday, and they had baked
matzoth, not according to all the strictures of the Plain, but
still they had made everything fit. The winter had been hard,
and the winds had plucked tiles off the roof, and the two of
them, at the height of the frost, had had to repair what could
be fixed. Hardest of all had been the collapse of the barn.
They had saved the cow from the ruins and, having no choice,
they had quartered it in one of the bedrooms.

The cemetery was lit up by the sun. The night rains had
watered the earth, and, despite the lateness of the hour, the
moist odor of weeds still wafted up from the gravestones.
Seven years ago they had arrived there. Then too the day had
been high and bright, and Uncle Arieh had stood at the door
of the house, raised both his arms, and said, "It's good that
you've come." His face was broad and pockmarked, and he
had then seemed, at first glance, to be a judge hewn from the
Bible. During the few days they had stayed with him, he had
taught them lessons in construction, irrigation, plowing, and
harrowing. About matters of faith he barely spoke. Once Gad
had asked him what one does when one loses track of time.
"Nothing," was his surprising answer. Afterward he corrected himself and said, "You go down below, stop a wagon,
and ask." He spoke little, to the heart of the matter, and
without ornament. They were not used to that kind of
speech, and they were perplexed. Later he had shown them

the peak. He did not raise his voice or use any exceptional word. He did not even quote a single verse. Gad had been astonished in his soul that a man who had lived for years in the company of holy tombs wouldn't speak even a single word out of the Bible. Now he clearly remembered the robust expression of his uncle's face, the way he sat straight in the straw-cushioned chair, as though he had not gone to his eternal rest but rather still sat and looked at the peaks as they gradually grew darker in the evening.

The next morning, as though they had risen from a deep pit, the first pilgrims appeared, a group of tall, lean people. Before them stepped two boys dressed in long linen tunics. The boys looked, perhaps because of their erect gait, like gentile choirboys. Gad, who had intended to ask for payment immediately as they entered, was surprised and did not stop them. They overran the place, without asking permission or offering a word of greeting, and then headed straight for the cemetery.

When he had recovered somewhat he let Limzy off his chain, clipped a short leash to his collar, and went toward the cemetery too.

"Where are you going?" Amalia tried to delay him.

"Don't you see?"

"What am I to do?" she cried out loud.

"Watch over the house. That's all," he said and ran out.

Amalia shuttered the windows, lit the lantern, and went down to the cellar.

When he reached the cemetery the people were already scattered among the tombstones, praying and weeping. The two boys stood near the entrance gate. Earnestness clung to their features, as though they were about to start singing.

"Where do you come from?" One of the lean men addressed Gad.

"What do you mean? This is my place," Gad said out loud.

"You have property rights?"

"Dating back five generations."

"I've heard a lot about the place, but I myself am here for the first time."

"How did you get here?"

"By foot."

"There weren't any wagons?"

"We were afraid to enter the villages, because of the dogs they sicked against us."

"This dog is a good one," said Gad.

"I can see," the man replied, smiling.

The people scattered about reminded him of the summer before, but this time they seemed more miserable. That was evident in the women's faces. Their hair was gray and disheveled, as only grief will affect a person's hair.

"What happened in the Plain?" Gad asked the man standing at his side.

"A typhus epidemic has spread through the entire area. People are dying like flies."

"What can one do?" asked Gad, immediately regretting his question.

"People do everything and nothing at all," said the man, smiling again.

"And who suggested that you come here?" asked Gad in the gray voice of a storekeeper.

"What do you mean, who? Is there any more holy place? If the gates of heaven do not open here, where will they be opened? You tell me." The man's voice drew him on.

In the past healthy people had also joined the pilgrims, people who had not been tried by afflictions, in solidarity with the sufferers. They used to give to charity and take care of the elderly. At the end of the visit something of the sadness of the sufferers would also cling to them. This year no one like that was to be seen. Grief was stamped on all faces, and it was clear they had not only come to pray but also to tear open the tombs, to awaken the fathers from their sleep so they would defend babes who had not sinned. At one time Gad too had been involved in those prayerful struggles, participating and helping, but this time murky selfishness swamped him, and he looked at them from a distance as though they were not brothers in sorrow.

A woman, no longer young, dressed in a long buttoned dress, approached him and said, "That dog frightens me."

"I'm holding him tightly on the leash," Gad replied.

"All the way, dogs molested us. I thought that here I'd find a moment of repose."

"Who will guard this place?" Gad raised his voice.

"Do the martyrs need to be guarded?"

"A cemetery is a cemetery. If one doesn't guard it, the

fence will collapse, the tombstones will fall down, and the place will fall prey to crows and wolves. Don't you understand that?''

The woman bent her head as though reprimanded and asked, ''The dog won't bite me?''

''I promise you,'' he said without looking at her.

At first he had it in mind to open the synagogue, but he didn't open it. He took the alms box out of the back room, stood at the gate, raised the heavy box, and in the voice of a gravedigger he proclaimed, ''Charity will save you from death.'' He immediately put the container down at the gate and stepped back a little. Limzy uttered a few clipped barks. The people were alarmed but didn't flee. The women prayed in Yiddish, mentioning the names of the sick and asking mercy for them. No one stepped up to the alms box to slip a coin into it.

Thus it had been the year before, as well. No one had bothered asking how one lived here. Where does the firewood come from? The food? Who drives away the vandals so they won't profane the graves? He was almost about to raise the box and shout, Without charity there can be no redemption. Whoever doesn't give charity, Limzy will drive him off!

That very moment one of the old men rose and called out, ''Children, afternoon prayers.'' Everyone rose from where they were lying and went out to the clearing to stand and pray. Gad did not join the worshipers. He stood at the side and looked at them, and the more he watched, the more anger flooded him. Without delaying another moment, he turned and went away.

When he reached the house, he found the door locked and

the windows shuttered, and a suspicious silence lay all about. He immediately pounded on the door with his fist and shouted, "Open up!" For some reason it seemed to him that the man with whom Amalia had conversed two years ago had sneaked in, and now they were copulating in the bed. When she was slow to open, he pounded, this time with both fists.

"Who's there?" he heard a panicked voice.

"It's me."

Amalia opened the door. Her face was wrapped in darkness, and a kind of foolish smile hovered on her lips.

"What have you been doing?" he asked like a peasant.

"Nothing at all. I was in the cellar."

"How come?"

"I was frightened."

"And you didn't prepare lunch?"

She hid her face in both hands. Now it seemed to him that she was about to cry.

He immediately changed his tone and said, "No one bothered to slip a cent into the alms box. I left the box in the middle of the gateway, so they can't say they didn't see it."

"Didn't you say anything?" asked Amalia in a frightened voice.

"They are busy with themselves," he answered in a gentile voice.

"I'm glad," she said, and the foolishness returned to her face.

"We should have stopped them at the gate."

"Correct," she said, and she knew that with that word she had won his heart.

Later, when he had consumed the meal, his face relaxed. The thought that the people had not discovered her pregnancy was comforting to him, as though he had managed to delude them. After the meal he did not return to the cemetery, as was his habit. He leaned on the wall, beside the shuttered windows, as though he were standing in order to hear the noises outside.

"Why don't we have a drink?" he said.

"Right away," she said, glad he wasn't scolding her.

After a few drinks he sank to his knees and said, "I felt very bad."

"Why?" She wanted to draw close to him.

"I was afraid of them."

"There's nothing to be afraid of. I'll go straight to Moldovitsa. The gentile crones will take me in. No one there asks where you come from or where you're going. It's a pretty place."

This was the first Gad had heard about the plan, and he was shocked. He too knew who went there and for what purpose. "It's a Christian place."

"Only a woman can understand another woman's sorrow." She remembered a saying she had heard in her childhood.

"You should go to Jews and not to Christians." He spoke without meaning it.

"The old women in Moldovitsa know just what has to be done. They are experienced, and there's nothing to fear."

"And you won't come back here?"

"I don't know."

"As for me," he said, "this place is stifling."

"And where do you want to go?" She chuckled for some reason.

"I swore to Uncle Arieh. Were it not for that oath, I would renounce my claim to the place."

She knew he was lying, but she didn't make any comment. Later, Limzy's hoarse barks were heard outside.

"He misses Mauzy," said Amalia.

"How do you know?"

"He never barked that way before."

"Dogs have short memories," he said, but he himself, as though in spite, now remembered Mauzy's stiff carcass and the two bare fangs, and a shiver passed down his body.

CHAPTER 24

That night they drank slowly, but a lot. The slivovitz kindled his imagination, and he spoke about a high wall that would surround the peak. Entry would be granted only to a few, not to sick people anymore, nor to those who had been in contact with the sick. There are enough cemeteries in the area, and they mustn't dump all their troubles in one place. Entry would be granted to quiet people, who don't raise a hubbub, and who don't mix into other people's lives, but who pray quietly, and without unnecessary contortions, and who return home after their prayers.

For some reason it seemed to Amalia that her big brother was now secretly preparing a roomy hiding place beneath the earth, a hiding place where they could raise their little daughter. In the warm, dark summer nights they would take her out and rock her in a cradle in sight of the stars. Amalia wanted to ask for details about the place, but she immediately grasped that the time was not yet ripe, and it would be better to wait.

Later his spirits fell, and he spoke about the dark Plain, the crowding and the bitterness and the sickness that ferment in every house. Therefore all the little towns had to be destroyed and the people had to be scattered across the hills. In the hills there is no crowding. Everybody can live by himself, and the air is fresh. All the anger that had been laid up in him for years now found words, phrases, and images, and his mind was not at ease until he had called typhus a Jewish fever.

That night Amalia too chimed in. She spoke about gigantic mothers who cruelly beat their tiny daughters. Gad knew she was talking about their mother, and for a moment he was about to say, It's forbidden to disturb the rest of the dead, but he was charmed by her voice. She spoke with eloquence, choosing words she hadn't used for years, and she was not satisfied until she had said, "It's wrong to keep women in dark grocery stores. Darkness darkens the soul, and when the soul is dark, hands beat without mercy." She immediately took off her blouse and showed him the scars on her hips and her left breast. Gad remembered the sight of the strap their mother used to beat them with, and he was filled with dread. It seemed to him she wasn't accusing their mother, but rather him, for doing what he did, and now he was trying to shake off his deeds.

"Put on your blouse. Don't catch cold." He walked over to her.

"It's not cold. I wanted to show you, so you wouldn't think I'm making it up."

He was familiar with that scar and loved it, but now he was afraid of it and also afraid she might go too far and do something violent. Her eyes glowed, and her hands were clenched in fists.

"Still, it is cold." He spoke to her softly. To his surprise she bared her right hip and said, "This hurts too. All winter long that scar hurt me. I didn't want to tell you, but it hurt me a lot." Gad knew that scar as well, but now for the first time he saw how pink it was.

"Mother did all that to me with her own hands. I didn't kill her babies. They died of typhus."

"It's hard to understand that," he muttered.

"It's not hard to understand. She wanted to kill me."

"You mustn't talk that way."

"Why shouldn't I talk that way? It's the very truth."

"It will heal." He spoke without conviction.

"Can't you see that it's an open scar?" She raised her voice.

"But Father loved you." He was glad in his heart that she didn't blame him.

"People who pray feel mercy for others."

"Mother used to pray too." He tried to defend her for a moment.

"Not the prayer of self-abnegation. Her two feet stood firmly planted on the ground. She even used to get angry at Father."

"It was all for our sake." He tried to shunt the tempest

aside, but his last words fanned the blaze even more. She was pretty in her nakedness that night and spoke with great power, as though she were speaking not only of her own indignities but also about all her friends who had been abused by bitter parents and domineering husbands. It was evident she was prepared to open the door and go outside to show everyone the burning scars on her body.

"Put on your dress. Why won't you put on your dress?" He approached her.

"I'm not afraid, and I'm not ashamed." Her voice was not her own.

"Typhus is raging outside," he said for some reason.

"That doesn't concern me, that doesn't concern me." She made a dismissive gesture with her hand.

Later they were both drunk. Amalia spoke about another life, a full life, without shame or fear, and Gad promised her that the wall around the peak would be high. No one would enter, only a few, only the select. At the same time she wanted him to swear he would never marry another woman in her place, and he, indeed, swore out loud.

Afterward their words no longer had meaning. She spoke about Mauzy's beauty and loyalty and about his imminent resurrection. Gad knew he should warn her and reprimand her, but he himself was completely blurry and collapsed on the floor. Nevertheless he still caught her cry: "He will be resurrected, you'll see!"

CHAPTER 25

The next morning, when he woke up and stood on his feet, Amalia was still plunged in deep sleep. He gave water to Limzy, tended the cow, and milked it. The silence was huge, and he forgot the pilgrims' presence on the peak. When he came back, he lit the stove, took the butter out of the pantry, and spread it on a slice of bread. Amalia slept on her back, her hands spread out on the large cushion, and it was clear that she would sleep for many more hours.

He had it in mind to go to the vegetable beds and check whether they had to be watered, but he remembered that the pilgrims were now scattered over the cemetery. He immediately set aside everything else and hurried over there. On his way he remembered what they had done to him the year before. They had dirtied the clearing and the outhouse, and not even the well, not even it, had they spared. If only they might leave me and observe my Torah, a forgotten verse rose up in his mind. Once one of those marvelous old men, Reb Pinchas, had greatly moved him with his sermons. Since then years had passed, and in the meantime the old man had gone to his eternal rest.

Now he saw Amalia with different clarity. Her naked body that night had been full and tender, and the scars added a secret attraction. Her breasts were large but not sagging. She had walked about the room as though she had finally managed to free her tethered wings, and she indeed floated. When he had sworn to her that he would not marry another woman in her place, she said to him, "It's nice that you swore," and she had patted him on the shoulder mischievously. Her pregnancy wasn't visible, perhaps because she walked erect. Sometimes she would go over to him so he could caress her, and he would. Toward morning she had spat out a few clear sentences. He remembered one of them: "You have nothing to worry about. I'll go to Moldovitsa, and I'll take care of everything there. If I don't come back, that will mean I've gotten lost." Now he was certain she had said, "gotten lost." He was annoyed that he hadn't scolded her.

In the clearing near the cemetery the people sat leaning against the fence. Their faces were encrusted with bewilderment, as though they had returned from a long journey but without any merchandise. Their goods had been stolen, and the horses too. As though now the wagons were standing empty at the side of the road. Gad ignored them. His thoughts were given to the alms box. The box was lying where he had left it the day before. He was sure that this time no one would slip a cent into it either, and when fall came he would again have to sell one of the possessions left them by Uncle Arieh. He stepped over to the box, intending to raise it and announce, There is no such thing as an unpaid guardian in this world. Anyone who doesn't contribute right away will be ejected. I've been exploited for seven years now. Without my inheritance I would have starved to death. True, I'm not a saint like Uncle Arieh, but I do my job conscientiously. I only ask to be paid as a guard.

He leaned over and gripped the handle of the box and immediately felt that the large old box was full to the brim. For a moment he wanted to raise it and clutch it to his chest, but his fingers felt as though they were burning, and he left it in place and withdrew.

"What's this?" He blurted out the words. "This is too much." Years before, when he was still a child, one of the regular customers had come into the store and handed him a silver coin, saying to him, "This is for you and your sister Amalia. Divide it equally. Last night I dreamt about you, children, and I swore to myself that if I awoke safe and sound I would give you a silver coin." Then as now he had said, "This is too much," and withdrawn.

Later he approached the people and called out, "I'm opening up the synagogue." Hearing his call, they all rose to their feet. The tall woman who had spoken to him the day before approached him and asked, "Are we going to the martyrs' synagogue?"

"Correct. It is also called From the Depths, because you go down seven steps to enter it."

"I didn't know," said the woman and bent her head.

Gad told her that on the day of the pogrom the martyrs had taken refuge there, but it was a harsh siege, and the little water they had was not enough to sustain them while they dug a tunnel.

"I didn't know," murmured the woman. "I didn't know."

They all went down, and Gad asked them to step forward and sit next to the Holy Ark. They immediately began afternoon prayers. The familiar whispers surrounded him on all sides, and he knew it had been months since he had prayed. The letters had been erased from his head, and it was doubtful whether an open prayerbook would still be of any use to him.

After the prayers he wanted to serve the worshipers coffee, as Uncle Arieh had done, but he had not prepared any. If Amalia hadn't cleaned it in time, the place would have been neglected. Nevertheless he recovered his wits and lit the stove, placed a pot on it, and went out to fetch coffee. Amalia was alarmed by his hasty return and asked, "What's the matter?"

"Good people came this time. They filled the alms box to the brim."

Amalia smiled as though she had been caught out improperly dressed.

Gad served them coffee, and they sang the hymn "Eternal Lord" to a sad melody. The melody flowed into the evening lights. The old men had not come this time, and the prayers sounded meager and clipped. There was one old fellow who

looked outwardly like the old men, but he didn't seem to
have their fire. He sat bent over, and it was evident that his
old age oppressed him. After the prayers no one gave a sermon. Everyone went outside and stood by the door of the
synagogue. Uncle Arieh had warned him not to allow the
people to stay too long in the cemetery, because too long a
stay there became a cult of the dead; he said he should bring
the people to the synagogue, since study was as effective as
prayer, and he interpreted the well-known verse for him, "A
Sage is preferable to a prophet." Gad did not remember the
interpretation. He did not heed that warning. He himself was
more and more drawn to the cemetery. If he found a time of
satisfaction in this severe silence, it was only the hours he
spent in the cemetery. The synagogue always afflicted him
with melancholy. Later the old man recovered, rose, and
gave a sermon on the verse "The heavens are the heavens of
the Lord, and the earth He gave to sons of man." He warned
them against questioning, and he spoke out for action, because action is body and soul wrapped up together. If someone acts, his prayers are granted, and he is shown meaning
too. Probing and self-scrutiny were the scourges of the time.
Only in full action is a man planted in both worlds.

Again they sang doleful songs and songs of longing. The
women wept. Thus it was every year. There were years when
they used to sit for entire nights, praying and singing, and in
the morning Gad would find them curled up in the clearing,
everyone in his own corner, like a defeated camp. Uncle
Arieh had also warned him against that unacceptable practice,
but he himself had been drawn into the night songs, and

sometimes he had fallen down together with the rest and slept where he was.

After the song, Gad announced out loud, "We have two free rooms. If anyone needs the shelter of a roof, let him come." No one asked. In the cemetery clearing they lit bonfires and hurriedly prepared supper. For a moment they too forgot that down below a dreadful epidemic was raging, a cruel epidemic, which was slaughtering children and old people. Some of the pilgrims went out to gather twigs while others fanned the flames.

When he returned to the house, he found Amalia sitting with a bottle. Her eyes were burning, and she wasn't drunk. Gad opened the alms box and emptied it carefully. The box contained gold and silver coins, pins and rings, and two pairs of earrings. He had never seen such a full alms box. Amalia's happiness was of a different sort. She hugged the empty box and murmured, "What a treasure, what a treasure!" Gad sat and carefully sorted out the gold, silver, and copper coins. He placed the jewelry in a plate. After sorting and making a reckoning, he said in a strange voice, "This will last us for at least two years." A foolish smile spread on his face, like an overgrown child who has finally gotten what he wanted.

Later at night, after eating and drinking, he told her enthusiastically that the pilgrims who had come this time were restrained and quiet and didn't make a hubbub, that they had to be helped, because their tragedy was grave. "If we can make things easier for them, we will have done a very good deed." Amalia sat opposite him and hugged the alms box with both hands, and her eyes glittered with cold joy. Gad was frightened by her look, but he continued to warn her that it was wrong to leave sick and old people beneath the open sky. The nights were cold and damp, and toward the morning fierce winds blew. Amalia did not take her eyes from him. In the end she burst out in thick laughter, wild laughter, and lay down on the floor.

The next day the sky was dark, and a gloomy cloud hovered over the peak. "We mustn't sleep in the house while people are sleeping outdoors," he murmured distractedly. It was nine o'clock, and Amalia was still deeply sunk in sleep. During the past few days her face had been tense, and she had remained in the cellar most of the day. He had the idea of taking her to the clearing and the synagogue, but he immediately realized that the disgrace, if it were revealed, would be great. He had concealed the coins and jewelry in a hiding place the night before. Now the solid alms box stood empty on the table. The remorse that had seethed within his chest all night long was now reduced to a single sentence: "This time too I have deceived the innocent."

When he returned to the clearing, everybody was sitting near the fence. The muddy light of the heavens made the people's faces gray. Gad regretted that he had not asked forgiveness the day before. Now if he asked them to pardon him, they wouldn't know what for. Everyone was awaiting the old men, but they were slow to arrive. Their lateness cast a harsh fear of heaven upon the people.

One of the men approached him and asked, "When will the old men come?"

"Soon," Gad answered energetically. "No year passes without the old men. The trip is hard for them, but they come."

Hearing those words the man bowed his head and thanked him. That bowing of the head revealed, inadvertently, the tattered lining of his coat and the patches he had sewn in a vain effort to mend it. Most of the coat linings here were tattered, but such a gaping lining Gad had never seen in his life. When he stepped aside he noticed that the back of the coat was puffy, and the patch was pulled all the way up inside it, holding together the belt and extending up to the collar. The patch running the length of the coat now seemed to him like a concealed spring that burdened the man's back.

The man said in resignation, "We need the old men as we need air to breathe." It was evident that he had prepared the cliché in advance, and now he was pleased it had left his mouth.

"We must wait patiently, and we mustn't hasten the end." Gad spoke with conviction.

Upon hearing those words, a smile spread across the man's face, and he said, "What can we do? Time presses on in any event."

Gad knew the man was talking about the death that had

settled within him and in his clothing, and if the old men didn't come, evil spirits would vanquish the angels.

"It's too bad. We thought we would find them," he said, like someone who has missed more than his chance.

The two boys sat on the side, and from their large eyes flowed a kind of fierce wonderment.

"Where are the boys from?" Gad asked as though he had just discovered them.

"They're twins," the man quickly replied. "Their parents and brothers died in the epidemic. We were afraid to leave them alone."

"It's good you brought them." Gad spoke with a kind of dreadful practicality.

"They're quiet, and they pray."

"The old men will come and bless them," said Gad, and he immediately sensed that his words were shallow.

Two women sat next to the large tombstone whose letters had been effaced, and they prayed silently. A few years earlier, a venerable old man, Reb Mordecai, had read the erased parts of the inscription out loud. Now no one remembered what had been worn away. The day before he had already noticed that the women were sitting next to the high tombstone and praying.

"We have two vacant rooms, and it's possible to house the women and children there." Gad spoke emotionally.

"We cannot stay for a long time. They're waiting for us down below."

"Rain will fall soon. You mustn't leave the women out in the open."

"Last night we slept in the synagogue. It wasn't cold." The man spoke apologetically.

"We have two wide beds in each room, a well, and a bathroom. This is an hour of trial for us too."

"You mustn't let us into the house. We are sick people." The man spoke with a frightening voice.

"I'm not afraid." He took courage. "Jews don't frighten me. Jews are responsible for one another, as we have said for all these years. The time has come to call in that debt."

At that time three men sat in the synagogue and studied books. Their cheeks were marked with yellow, and their fingers trembled on the pages.

"Blessed be those who study," Gad called out loud.

They drew their eyes up from the books, and the yellow glowed on their faces as though they were illuminated from afar. "Has the epidemic even come here?" one of them asked and immediately regretted his question.

"Here the winter was long and hard. No one came and no one went. The snow reached the top of the houses."

"Are you alone here?"

"My sister and I," he answered, and immediately felt that the stranger's eyes had pierced his secrets.

"When does spring reach here?" the man asked, as though asking about something hidden.

"Very late. After the Feast of Weeks. Sometimes there's no summer here at all. Two years ago the snow didn't melt until Tammuz, and it immediately came back anew. We aren't our own masters here." Gad was glad the man wasn't touching on his personal life anymore.

"All these years we haven't been here. Only now we remembered to come. This is a marvelous place." The man spoke with elation.

"What do you do in that long darkness?" The other man raised his eyes from the book and asked clearly.

"I saw wood. My hands never stop feeding the stoves."

"And you never get angry, so you want to leave everything behind and go down below?"

Gad was flustered by the question, but he recovered himself and replied, "One mustn't leave this place unguarded. Sometimes the snow melts, and with enormous power it sweeps away everything that stands in its way. Someone has to be here, isn't that so?"

"Correct," the man said in a prosecutor's tones.

"Someone has to keep watch," he emphasized.

"Is there a lot of ice here?" the man asked for some reason.

"A great deal. In the winter the whole mountain is ice, one big block. We've been guarding this place for many generations already. Now it's fallen to my lot. I'm not complaining. On bright days the visibility is clear, and the Plain lies before us as though on our palm. These graves are very precious, and a person feels at home here."

Now all three of them raised their eyes and looked at him. The yellow on their faces paled, and they seemed like men immersed in a deep vision.

"I didn't want to disturb you," said Gad and withdrew slightly.

Now the yellow color returned to their faces, and Gad told them that three years ago there had been a bad epidemic, and many people had come up to ask for mercy. The old men tore the firmament, and the epidemic had been halted.

"When will the good old men come?" asked one of them, and a sigh of pain was torn from his chest.

When he returned to the house that night, he didn't tell Amalia a bit of what his eyes had seen. For a long while he stood by the water barrel and washed his hands. Amalia served him hot soup, cheese pie, and borscht. The food was fragrant and savory, and Gad ate with an appetite. The people's tortured faces gradually faded from his mind, and he was glad he was alive and that the food was tasty.

CHAPTER 27

The next day cold rain fell, and Gad stood at the entrance of the synagogue and asked the people to come and take shelter in his house. The thought that he was capable of doing an important good deed filled his soul with the desire to act. But no one was quick to say, I'm coming. Fear that the rain would trap them up above gave them a miserable look. Some of them approached Gad and asked whether there was a shortcut to the villages, and others asked about the villagers' disposition. Gad's mind was distracted, and he spoke about the frost and about the dampness that creeps into the marrow of one's bones, and said it was preferable, for the moment, to sit and wait, and better in a closed house next to a warm stove.

Morning prayers did not allay the panic. The clouds that had settled on the peak and the rain that came in its wake strengthened the feeling that if the old men had not come yet, it meant the epidemic had not halted. Everyone there was trying to do the impossible, and it would be better to hurry back down. Who could know what the angel of death was achieving?

Where are the old men, where are they? the eyes implored. Every year those stubborn human skeletons stood and aroused the heart, shredding fear to bits. Only when fear is uprooted is there a place for faith. For faith a tranquil soul is needed. Now the peak seemed to be wrapped in swirling fog, as though the earth had been removed from beneath it, and the people were like gnarled knots of fear. Who are we and what is our life here? Why don't we go down to save what it's possible to save? They groped like blind men. Years before, carried on a stretcher, a paralyzed old man had arrived at this season. The old man could barely talk, but his devotion to the place was clear and evident to everyone. He addressed the saints and called them by their names, and the people saw with their own eyes; heaven was no longer blocked off. It was possible to open up and speak to it. Since then many old men had come, and they too, each in his own way, showed miracles.

At night, as the cold grew more intense, the women and two children agreed to come and take shelter in the house. Amalia was embarrassed, and in her great shame she mumbled, "Please come in, the house is empty." The two stoves rumbled as in the winter, and Gad hurriedly sliced the large loaf of bread. Amalia poured coffee in pottery cups, and the women gripped the cups and sipped thirstily.

"When will the old men come?" a woman asked with a trembling voice.

"They must come." Gad spoke in a voice not his own.

"Sick children are waiting for us below."

"The old men have come here even at times when the army blocked the way. Someone always brings them."

Upon hearing that answer, a smile spread on the woman's face, as though he had told her a secret.

The next day the sky cleared, and a large pale sun appeared in the heaven. Everyone went out and stood in the clearing, and there was a feeling, which Gad shared, that in a short while many good folk would come, and they would bring the old men with them. The people went out to gather twigs, and they lit two bonfires. The smell of the twigs and the smell of coffee restored the place's firm status: here it was possible to pray and not give in. If one didn't give in, there was hope. A person climbing cliffs must never despair, not even for a second.

After prayers Gad brought fresh rolls and cherry jam. Amalia had baked all night long. Toward morning her face glowed from the fire of the furnace, and she muttered words that sounded like spells. Gad did everything in haste, with a kind of compulsive diligence, and as he worked he implored the people not to descend too soon, for now that the weather had improved, no doubt the old men would not be long, and they mustn't miss out on their blessing.

Again a day passed and the old men did not come. People's minds were made up more and more strongly that if they did not arrive by the evening, there would be no choice but to descend. Gad brought out two bottles of slivovitz and poured drinks for the men. They made the blessing and drank, and suddenly a kind of fury grew on their faces, but the women, loyal to the place, did not move from the graves and prayed in whispers. The boys stood at the gate, and their faces expressed wonderment. Gad brought them cheese cake and cups of milk, and they ate and said grace. When he returned to the house in the evening, he found the door open and Amalia lying in bed. For a moment he clenched his fingers angrily, and he was about to call out, What's the matter, what's this self-indulgence? but when he saw her face, pale and weak, he asked softly, "How are you feeling?"

"I feel very dizzy, and I vomit all the time."

"If only I knew what to do now," he said and turned to the stove. He poured himself a cup of coffee, and for a long time he sat quietly.

At night she felt better and spoke about the mountaintop with great emotion, as though it weren't an exposed place, thrown upon the mercies of the wind, but rather the village of her childhood, where people and animals grow together, where the grain turns golden in the summer, and in the winter it is hot and pleasant in the houses, and only when a person is sick is he uprooted from those wonders and taken down to the city, to the hospital or the sanctuary.

"That's it." She accepted the verdict.

"But you'll come back." He had to say that.

"With God's help," she said, and for a moment she confided her life to the hands of the Creator of life.

Gad was scared by that submissiveness and said, "I still don't see you going."

The next day the sky's clarity persisted, and everyone knew they had to get down from the mountain promptly. The boys' long linen tunics had gotten dirty, and their faces were ruddy from the sun. Now they no longer looked like polite choirboys but like two tired shepherds who had found a moment to rest under a tree. In vain Gad tried to delay them. After prayers they headed hastily for the slope. Gad watched them as they went away. He was angry that they hadn't taken their leave of him or thanked him. Immediately afterward he became depressed and sat in the empty clearing. It seemed to him those people had uprooted some great feeling from his heart, and now the feeling was absent, the meaning of life had been taken away. When he returned to the house he found Amalia sitting outdoors. Her face was quiet, and she smiled at him.

"Their patience was at an end, and they didn't want to wait anymore," he said.

"They have sick children at home."

"All of us need the old men's blessing."

"Correct," Amalia said, as though she had been reminded of an important principle.

Inwardly he was pleased that she wasn't talking about traveling to Moldovitsa. Her face was as full as formerly, and Gad remembered the winter now and its sharp sweetness, and the darkness that had isolated them from the world and its tumult. A kind of dark yearning washed over his body, as though the sky were about to close up again.

"Amalia," he said.

"What?"

"I wonder whether anyone else will come."

"They'll come."

"How do you know?"

"A warm wind is blowing outside, and it always brings people."

Toward the High Holy Days many people came from the cities, the towns, and the villages, enough for about three prayer quorums, with peddlers clinging to them, along with some charlatans and a few cripples who made a living from their deformities. A money changer who had not shown himself on the mountaintop for years was not offering money now but army boots. His face was reddened by the sun, and he looked healthy, carefree, as if he'd completed a military service unharassed. No one looked at his merchandise, but he didn't rant. As if in spite, he smoked fine cigarettes and looked at the people with a kind of tranquility. The old men hadn't come, and people stood by the tombs as if abandoned. In the summer it had seemed the epidemic was about to halt, and indeed there were many indications to that effect. But this turned out to have been merely a lull. At the end of the summer it raged mercilessly.

God, remove this dreadful plague from us, for Thou art our father, and we have no father or protector but Thee.

The people were silent next to the graves, but there were women who could not restrain themselves, and they cried out, "Where are the old men? Where are those marvelous high spirits who know how to pray, how to thunder at the world, and how to keep silent when you have to keep silent? Where are those wonderful men? Why have they abandoned us?"

Gad stood at their side but didn't know how to help them. He and Amalia baked rolls, and in the morning they served everything they had prepared for the needy. The cow's milk dwindled, but the little there was sufficed for the sick and the children. The people were sunk in their grief and accepted what was served to them without thanks. However, their muteness did not weaken him. Now for some reason he was certain that this was the way they must behave. Needy people who give thanks with every step they take are like beggars. When someone is grieving, his grief conquers him, and one must accept him as he is.

Now his life was settled and well paced. He would rise early, light the stoves, fodder the cow, prepare coffee, and immediately rush over to take part in morning prayers. After prayers he would work for an hour or two in the garden. The carrots and cauliflower were coming up nicely, and the tomatoes blushed red. He would bundle together a few vegetables, wash them, and take them to the clearing. Amalia, for her part, spared no effort. She cooked and baked, as in a wealthy household laden with guests, until late at night. The icy immobility of her life thawed out, but she did not attain happiness. Everything she did was done with a kind of tension.

Sometimes they would work in shifts. When Amalia sank down on her cot at night, Gad rose. Thus day followed day. Amalia did not complain. Now she did many of the things she had intended to do all those years. She cleaned out the cellar and the attic and planted bushes next to the fence around the house. "A bare fence isn't pretty," she said. Now, among other things, she fulfilled that small wish.

Sometimes in the middle of the night a kind of sigh would moan out of the depths in the darkness and set the peak trembling. Gad knew these were longings for the old men and pains for which there is no balm, someone's desperate effort to summon the holy patriarchs on his own, so they would act where necessary and without delay. In those dark hours the distant epidemic would take on the tortured features of Aunt Sarah, their father's sister who had died in her youth of a typhus epidemic that felled many young people one winter.

But meanwhile bad news came from the Plain. A pogrom had broken out in the town of Halintsa, and the mob had plundered it. Though a few families managed to flee, most of them were caught in their sleep. The bad news came with two thin men whose look was more eloquent than the words they brought.

As always: What shall we do? Where shall we go? It was impossible to fight on two fronts. Having no other escape, they threw themselves down on the graves and implored.

The sight of the people next to the graves recalled other times and pogroms. In truth, there was never a year without pogroms. This year the mob and the epidemic had worked in tandem. The money changer, who had sat next to the fence all that time, expressionless, smoking fine cigarettes, as though the common cause had nothing to do with him, suddenly gave out a strange shout. First it appeared that he was lowering the price of his military boots so as to sell them. The strange shout was repeated with a force conveying a request and also anger. Finally it turned out that he was calling to his wife, who had recently died and left him alone with five orphans. At first the people ignored his cries, but in the end, when they realized what was the matter, they approached him. He pushed them away, saying, "Don't mix in. You don't understand anything. You have no concept." He spoke like someone who had awakened from a deep sleep.

Before Rosh Hashanah fierce rains fell, and the people hastily left. Gad vainly entreated them to stay, saying it would be better to wait until the storm had passed. Their flight was strange. Amalia stood on the threshold and waved her hand with the expression of an abandoned soul. A few women approached her and hugged her and immediately turned their backs as though running away. Gad stood by the gate rigidly and saw them off on their descent.

When darkness fell he did not return to the house but rather turned and went to the clearing. Unlike previous years, the clearing was clean and without litter. Nothing remained even of the bonfires. It was as though people had not assembled here but rather passed by like the wind. The two acacia trees spread their bare branches and imperceptibly reminded him of the sturdy and mad face of the money changer.

When he returned home, darkness already hung on the peaks. Amalia was sitting by the extinguished stove, and her face expressed cold astonishment. "That's it," he said.

Hearing that grunt, Amalia bent her head.

"I told them, We have enough room. You can get sick from the damp."

"True," said Amalia distractedly.

"All serious diseases are caused by dampness. I told them, but they didn't want to listen to me."

Afterward the sky cleared, and on the horizon fiery furnaces flowed into the dark valley. The sight reminded him of the frosty days that were approaching. For some reason it seemed to him that Amalia was about to burst out crying.

He stood up and adjusted his voice. In artificial tones he said, "You mustn't sink into melancholy."

Amalia didn't respond. Her eyes were open with a kind of sharpness he hadn't noticed in her previously. The look said, Why are you wearying me with empty speech? Empty speech saddens me.

"What should we do, then?" he said, as though he had been asked.

"What?" said Amalia, as though she had just woken up.

"What could we have done that we haven't done, I'm asking."

"Why are you asking?" The sharp look returned and tensed her eyes.

"Have I made a mistake?" He retreated.

"This year you helped many good people." She spoke in a voice not her own and with words that were not hers.

"I'm ashamed," he answered, not to the point.

"You have no reason to be ashamed." Her eyes were open wide. "In a few days I'll go to Moldovitsa. I'll hire a room from one of the gentile women. They tend to women with mercy. You have nothing to worry about."

Gad lowered his head and put his face in his hands as though she had hit him on the head with a hammer.

After that the days were clear, and Gad worked in the orchard for many hours. When he returned to the house at night, his head was swollen and ruddy like one of the watermelons he carried in his rucksack. Amalia worked too, cleaning the house and preparing hot meals. For hours they would sit by the window and consume plate after plate. Occasionally in the evening a voice would burst out in the distance and shatter the silence. "Did you hear?" Amalia would ask, shocked.

"It's nothing. They're loading logs onto barges." He calmed her down, and the night would return to its pace.

Her pregnancy advanced, but it was not yet noticeable in her movements. She worked briskly and quietly, which made Gad forget that she was a wounded woman preparing herself for a long journey. At night he would remember the old men, and a sigh would escape his throat. It had been hard during the summer. The people were in despair and had fled. He had done everything diligently, but it had been a labor without blessing. He missed the old men, especially the silent ones, who did not reproach people but sat, clinging to the place, until one felt their silence was causing a stirring in one's body. Several years ago old Mordecai had blessed him, a silent blessing, without touching him. All that winter the blessing had hovered over his head, and although the winter had been hard and frightening, with both stoves roaring without respite, his mind nevertheless had been alert and without sadness. In the evenings he had studied *The Path of the Righteous,* and his sleep had been that of hard-working people.

Now Amalia clearly remembered the tall, noble woman whose husband and both her sons had been snatched away by the epidemic. She used to sit at the edge of the clearing and pray, and every time Amalia approached her to offer her a roll or a drink, she would raise her large eyes and say, "May the Lord bless you for your deeds." Once Amalia dared to ask her name. The woman, surprised, drew her face up from the prayerbook and said, "My daughter, I have but little hold onto this world."

"What's the matter?"

"My dear ones are already there, and I am preparing to go to them."

Amalia was stunned by her directness and simplicity. Now that woman once again appeared to her, as though descending steep slopes into the abyss.

No more people came, and the peak withdrew into silence. The harvest was abundant, and Gad brought wheelbarrows full of potatoes, onions, and beets from the field. Amalia cleaned the vegetables and stored them in the cellar. The orchard also produced a bounty of fruit. Gad brought in a crateful of late-ripening plums, and Amalia set about making jam. Her stance next to the copper pot was that of a young girl. The storm has passed, the nightmare is over, he wanted to cry out. Now the cold, clear autumn days will come, and we can sit quietly. That was a temporary diversion. Amalia reminded him that the day was rapidly approaching when she would have to travel to Moldovitsa.

"In a little while," he would say and dismiss her words with a strange gesture.

That autumn there were several thefts, and Gad went out with Limzy to circle around the mountaintop. We mustn't shut ourselves in, we mustn't fear. Shutting ourselves in encourages the thieves; it's better to go out and anticipate them. Limzy was alert and tense, and Gad was glad to go out on nightly patrols with him. When they returned the dog's eyes sparkled like those of a creature content with his lot. The patrols did have an effect. Limzy ran after the thieves and sank his teeth into one of them. On those nights Gad was like a soldier whose way of life has been stamped with the pattern of extended service. He loved the earth at night, the rustle of the breeze and the screeches of the birds of prey, but more than that he liked to lie down in a position he had dug out with his own hands, listening to the rustling of the trees and bushes together with Limzy.

Sometimes Amalia would be reminded of the people who had stayed there, and she said, "What are our miserable folk doing?"

"It's impossible to worry about the whole world." He would cut her off.

"What can I do? I see them all day long."

"What do you want to do? Should we leave everything behind and go down to them?"

Meanwhile their staples had run out, and Gad decided that next day he would go down to the village and lay in supplies for the cold season.

"Meanwhile I'll get everything ready for the trip."

"Where?"

"To Moldovitsa."

"I still can't figure that out." He spoke to her as though it were a matter of housekeeping.

"I must go down to Moldovitsa."

"Not now; by no means." He spoke with a stammer.

Later she said, "Still we have to lay in supplies for the cold seasons. They're on their way."

"I'm prepared to go down, but the same wagon can't take you down below. By no means."

"Why not?"

"Because it's a supply wagon, only for supplies."

"But I must get to Moldovitsa."

"Not now."

What could she reply? She said, "If that's your opinion, I won't contradict you."

The next day he went down. Amalia and Limzy stood at the door of the house and watched his descent. He went down the path next to the abandoned Christian cemetery. His stride was young, and the morning lights were pleasant to touch. When he was close to the slope, he raised his right hand and called out, "Goodbye until evening. I'll see you in the evening."

This, in fact, happened every year. In previous years other fears would fill her heart: the gentile women. She knew his weaknesses and used to be jealous and frightened. There were years when fear for his safety dissipated, and only jealousy seared her heart. This time it was different. It seemed to her that she was guilty for everything.

Afterward she sat at the window and sipped a few drinks. Her fears gradually dissolved, and sights from distant days flooded her eyes. After Uncle Arieh's sudden death, Gad had been full of youthful energy and faith, and he had promised himself to make an effort to study Talmud. Without Talmud, a Jew was disfigured. In his youth his father and several teachers had tried to teach him the easier tractates, but it had been no use. It was hard for him to grasp the complicated arguments. Then too he had known that without Talmud his life was flawed, but even that awareness hadn't opened his mind. But this time he had been resolved to learn it, no matter what. During the first summer on the mountaintop he had not parted from the men as they studied, and whenever he found someone studying, he approached him. In the end he had been mistaken. In places like this a person does not study but rather begs and prays for one's soul; one tries to arouse the dead forefathers and to tear open the firmament. Even the learned didn't study here. In the end he lost hope. Now Amalia remembered his efforts as though it had been her own efforts that had proved futile.

Late at night Gad returned from the Plain. From his disheveled features Amalia learned that the purchases had been successful. After making them he had sat in a tavern and downed several drinks, and after that he had gone to Sophia's house, lain with her, and whispered in her ear whatever he had whispered. Meanwhile the wagon driver unloaded all the sacks and packages, and Gad paid him with coins.

"You drank too much," she said when they were alone.

"I was cold."

"How did the buying go?"

"It wasn't easy this time." He concealed the truth from her.

"I was beginning to worry about you."

"There's nothing to worry about."

Your face tells me that after you drank in the tavern you went by Sophia's house, she was almost about to say to him.

"I'm very tired; the trip wore me out," he said and sat on a chair.

You promised me you wouldn't lie with her. At one time she had spoken to him like a woman betrayed.

"The trip was long and tiring." He spoke like a peasant trying to conceal his sins from his wife.

"Now you can rest." Something of the peasant in him clung to her too.

"Did you make something to eat?"

"I did."

Gad ate with a strong appetite as though he had worked all day in an open field. As he ate he told her about the grain and oil merchants who had tried to cheat him. His sunburned face, his coarse speech, gave him the look of a cunning old peasant. She was sorry for his awkward face, the way he slurped his soup, his unpleasant way of sitting, and the lies he scattered shamelessly. For a moment she was about to tell him, It doesn't suit you to talk that way. That's not the way a Jew talks. She sat at some distance from him, sipping drink after drink and examining every one of his movements.

Afterward, without any connection, her heart opened and she spoke about long days of oppressive solitude and nights of bitter darkness and about friends who had not stood the test of time, and about desires that sully the soul.

Gad sat stunned. He had not imagined so much anger was laid up in her heart. Finally he approached her and said, "What's the matter?"

"You won't understand me. You can't understand me."

"Why not?"

"Because you drank in the gentile tavern. Their cognac thickens your soul. You mustn't drink their cognac. It's a drink without any soul. It's a coarse-souled drink that burns up good thoughts."

Now Gad surprisingly remembered Amalia as a girl who wore a long poplin dress and laced shoes and would sit for hours in the narrow corridor they called the cellar. In those years she had had a rare beauty. Silence would envelop her face. Only occasionally did she open her mouth, and she would mainly utter monosyllabic words, unusual words that had the sound of thin glass. Now too it seemed she was uttering them, but the sound had become a stammer, as with the deaf.

"I want to go home." That utterance burst from her mouth. "The time has come to go home."

"Gladly." He grasped that used word and repeated it.

"I want to go back to Father. It's been a long time since I've seen him. We mustn't leave him alone."

"I'll get a wagon." He was scared.

"And what will you do?"

"I'll watch over the place until you return."

"I won't be able to return. Don't you understand I won't be able to come back?"

"Why not?"

"Because I'm dirty."

She sank to the floor, and the great blunt words were crushed together in her mouth, becoming a torrent of tears. In vain he kneeled down to calm her. Since he couldn't stop the flow of her weeping, he took the sacks that were leaning against the door and dragged them one by one down into the cellar.

CHAPTER 30

When he got up the next morning, he found Amalia already kneading dough and preparing big loaves of bread. The oven glowed and gave off a thick brown light. Gad felt fatigue in all his limbs, but he overcame it and went out to tend the cow. For some reason it had seemed to him that she would pester him about Sophia this time too, but to his surprise she said nothing. She was immersed in kneading the dough, and even when he returned from the barn she said nothing that could be interpreted as a reproach or a recrimination. He prepared a cup of coffee for himself and sat not far from her. Now her pregnancy was clear to see, but she worked erect, with steady motions, like a person who loves his work and doesn't spend his time idly.

"I'm going to the cemetery," he said.

"Go in peace." She gave him a strange blessing.

"I'll be back at noon," he said, surprised by her odd benediction.

With no further delay he took the hoe and left. Low clouds flowed across the peak and the visibility was poor. He had intended to go straight to the cemetery, but for some reason he turned to the side and went to the vegetable garden. The garden was empty already. A few heads of cabbage grew wild and gave off a smell of rot.

Now he remembered clearly the old trench he had dug to lay bare the potato tubers, which were a dull red and protruded from the earth like breathing organs, and how he had picked them one by one and placed them in the wheelbarrow, and how Amalia's face brightened at the sight of the laden barrow. And the beets too were heavy and saturated with juice this year. The harvest had lasted a week, and as it went on, it had seemed there was no end to the crops. For many days afterward he could still feel the clods of earth crumbling between his fingers. For years these silent plots had produced plentiful crops, and now it was as though a widowed sadness had come and slapped him in the face.

Without his noticing it, that sadness reminded him of the pilgrims' faces. Panicked fear of typhus had driven them out of their minds. The cry, Where are the old men? Where are they? once again echoed in his ears, stripped, frightened voices that continued to seek the gates of mercy.

Afterward the silence returned and covered the peak. The sky grew clear, and the smell of damp vegetation came to his nostrils and reminded him, unawares, of Sophia's bed. This time she hadn't complained that he had neglected her for a long time. She was relaxed, laughed a lot, and even made jokes about the Jews.

"The Jews bring me boxes of candy, always boxes of candy."

"I hate boxes of candy," Gad said.

"Me too," she said and made a face.

"Have there been Jews here recently?" He was curious.

"Sophia likes Jews. They're always nice to her." She spoke of herself in the third person, as though she weren't a woman but an institution. Within himself he had to admit that in the past few years the finest hours he had passed were on her couch. She was no longer young, she was moody, but with a stroke of her hand she still knew how to raise a tempest that tossed within him for many days afterward.

This time she was pleased with the gift he brought her: a bracelet decorated with semiprecious stones. He had found the bracelet in the attic, in one of Uncle Arieh's hiding places. He had occasionally considered selling it, but in the end he decided to give it to Sophia. Sophia was overjoyed, flattered him, stroked him, and whispered several pleasing compliments in his ear. Gad knew those were words she said constantly, but they were still pleasant. He had a fierce desire to sleep with her and knead her body all night long, but concern for Amalia was stronger, and he left her house while it was still twilight. Fortunately he happened upon an old peasant who was willing to take him to the peak. This time he didn't bargain with him, and the two of them loaded the sacks on the wagon. The old peasant knew what he had done at Sophia's place, and he didn't hide his disapproval. When he was young, he told Gad, the village elders used to beat whores in the market square, but now debauchery was everywhere. She and her like corrupted the youth, and no one protested.

Strangely, the peasant's reprimand didn't sway him. The few hours he had spent with Sophia were so intoxicating that even harsh words lacked the power to ruin the sweet memory. Only as they drew near to the mountaintop did he know that Amalia had worked all day without pause, and in the evening she had stood at the window many hours and waited for him. When night fell she had lit the stove and sat next to it.

At first he was sorry about her fears, but as he advanced, rage gripped him, like a soldier whose leave is finished: Once again now the dreary platforms, the trains loaded with masses of soldiers, and, in a little while, back to the trenches, to the lookouts, with no light and no solace.

Had it not been for those pleasant, earthy, generous parts of Sophia's body, the world would have been even darker. Nothing remained now of that marvelous earthiness except the cheap perfume, weak traces of which clung to his nostrils. It is also the way of odors to fade. Although the visit had been made only the day before, and her fingers, rather the memory of their touch, still fluttered on his back, it seemed to him that it had been a long time ago, not in a neglected village but in a city with gardens and fountains.

When he reached the cemetery the sky opened, and a bright light flooded the clearing. Words that had been hidden within him rose on his tongue, and he said, "Amalia is tormented, though she is innocent. I must redeem her from her torments." Those two sentences had already haunted him, and now he said them aloud as though he were speaking them in the ears of a tall man. When he raised his eyes he saw the money changer who had stood in the clearing and sold army boots. His eyes were open, and a crazy smile, saved for when everything is done and gone, gleamed in his eyes, something like Mauzy's smile when he made his last run around the mountaintop.

As his glance circled the clearing he noticed that two gravestones had been knocked down, and that Simcha Leifer's monument had been broken to pieces. When he entered the cemetery, the sight was even more appalling: vicious slogans had been smeared in red paint on some of the gravestones, saying in the gentiles' language, *Death to the Jews who are alive and a curse on the dead Jews*. The villains had done their dirty work only a few hours before. Damp air still rose from the overturned earth, and the paint was fresh. Gad put the hoe down on the ground and hid his face in both hands. As in a dream at night, his legs felt as if they were stuck in the damp earth and if he tried to take even a single step he would be unable.

Then he approached Reb Simcha Leifer's smashed monument. He knelt, picked up the fragments, and placed them next to one another. The hammer blows still sparkled on the broken stone. Now it seemed to him that buried life, life that is forbidden to be seen, had been revealed to him. He took off his coat and placed it over the fragments.

He soon noticed that the overturned gravestones had also been vandalized. The letters had been completely eroded from those two gravestones, and not even the old men knew what had been carved on them. He raised them, lifting them up the way you help a sick person sit up, to make his breathing easier.

When he returned to the house at noon he found Amalia sunk in sleep. A dark silence permeated the room. A calamity has befallen us, he was about to call out loud, but seeing her face, a face contracted in bad sleep, he restrained himself. He drew near her bed and, quietly, said, "Amalia."

Amalia opened her eyes all at once, raised her head, and asked, "What's the matter?"

Large loaves of bread, braided challoth, and rolls, which Amalia had baked that morning, lay on shelves. The smell of poppy seed hung in the air. The sight of the rolls on the shelves reminded him of the sight of the people who had run away from here a few days ago in panic. Then too Amalia had baked day and night.

"Who's there?" Amalia cried out from her sleep.

"Me."

"It seemed to me as if the stove was lit."

"Nothing is burning."

"Has something happened?"

"Why do you ask?"

"I dreamt that a pogrom had overrun the house."

"That was a dream, nothing."

Later, when she was roused from her sleep, sitting up, leaning on her arms, he told her that vandals had smashed Reb Simcha Leifer's tombstone and knocked over the two worn-down monuments. Upon hearing that bad news, she leaned her head to the side and a foolish smile wrinkled her lips.

Gad recognized that frightening smile, but he couldn't

contain himself this time, and he said, "There's nothing to be done. We have to repair the damage ourselves."

"Who did it?" she asked in surprise.

For a moment it seemed as if Amalia meant to treat him harshly and torment him because of Sophia. That was only in appearance. She was still tangled in the web of sleep, and the nightmare that had pursued her in her slumber still clung to her eyelids. Her pursed lips asked, "What's the matter? Why won't anyone tell me the truth?"

"Mauzy wouldn't have let them deface the holy tombs." Gad raised his voice. "Mauzy would have laid down his life." And it was clear to his sister that he was talking not about the dog but about his other being, the hidden one, which was not subject to the temptations of the moment but did everything honestly and with firm resolution.

In the afternoon, bent on their knees, together they scrubbed the defiled tombstones with rags soaked in kerosene. Amalia's face was concentrated, and a muscle twitched occasionally in her upper lip. Gad, for some reason, spoke ceaselessly about Mauzy. If he had been alive, he would have prevented this desecration. But the hand that had poisoned him was the hand that had shattered the tombstones, and now we can only take vengeance for his spilt blood.

Amalia did not listen to the fatuous rhetoric that bubbled from his mouth. All her efforts were given over to scrubbing, and the many words he uttered only deafened her ears. She was almost going to say to him, Enough words, my head is splitting, but Gad finally fell silent of his own accord.

After hours of energetic cleaning, pale patches shone on the defiled tombstones. They were very careful not to damage the letters, but the letters still were damaged, and Gad passed over the scrubbed places, touching them as one touches a wound. He placed a wooden frame around the fragments of the shattered monument, and, wondrously, it was still possible to read what was written on it. He was pleased, and he expressed his pleasure with an odd clap of his hands.

Amalia was silent the whole time. After she finished the work of scrubbing, she sat down next to the fence and leaned on it. Her face was red, and large beads of sweat shone on her forehead. Arrogance was reflected in her eyes, as though she had acquired superiority by dint of the work of her hands. I didn't shirk either, he was about to say, but didn't.

Later he said, "Now everything is in its place. Nothing has happened. If they dare to come back, I'll beat them."

Amalia raised her eyes and looked at him coldly. It seemed she was about to close her eyes and pray.

"I'm going back to the house," said Gad.

"I'll sit here for a while," she said.

"I'm going to prepare two lookouts. One next to the house and one here."

"Do as you wish," she said, in the voice of a woman encumbered with many children.

"I won't abandon this property." He spoke again with pathos.

Amalia looked at him without trust and said nothing.

"I'm going," he said and left.

When he reached the courtyard he walked straight over to Limzy. Limzy bounded toward him with leaps of joy. Gad gave him the end of a sausage and said to him, "Soon we'll go out."

Perhaps because of the unmade beds, the house seemed

abandoned. The smell of slivovitz mixed with the smell of kerosene stood in the air, and Gad remembered that not many hours ago he had poured out the two cans of kerosene. The doors of the stove were open, and cold darkness wafted out of its gaping interior.

Gad was frightened by the silent neglect. He went down to the cellar and brought up some dry logs and lit the stove. The fire seized the dry logs, and the smell of slivovitz stood out more. The thought that the day before Amalia had sat by the stove and drunk glass after glass aroused a kind of disgust in him. He stepped over to the window and opened it wide, saying, "Now that smell will get out of here." As he pronounced those words, he remembered his trip at night from the Plain, the thick darkness, and the old peasant's reprimand. He hadn't imagined the look of his face would reveal his secrets to Amalia.

He thought of making a cup of coffee and sitting by the window. At one time sitting by the window used to knit together his scattered soul after a day of labor, but the evening was growing grayer, and he knew he had to go out and prepare the foxholes. Without delay he took up the spade and set out for the hill across the way with Limzy. That was one of his favorite lookout spots. From there he could see the steep peaks and the slopes beneath them, and now, after the rains, they spread out green and silent.

It was clear to him that bright days would no longer return. Everything was stained and besmirched. Nor were his thoughts as before. A kind of hidden sadness gnawed at his chest. "Amalia," he called out, "I will work hard day and night and atone for my bad deeds. Don't you understand?"

After digging for an hour he managed to hollow out a proper foxhole. He entered it and checked the visibility. It wasn't limited. Broad expanses lay before him down to the Plain. "We'll sit here and lie in wait for them tonight." He spoke to Limzy and was pleased to have him close by.

Now he thought of heading for the clearing near the cemetery and preparing a foxhole there too, but he remembered Amalia's tense face and her cold expression, and he immediately rejected that idea.

While he was standing by the foxhole, he saw Amalia walking toward him, dressed in a brown dress. Her steps were young, as though she weren't bearing a child in her womb. He immediately decided to go out to her. Amalia noticed him and stood still.

"Amalia," he called out.

Amalia stood where she was without moving.

"I dug a foxhole up there, a deep and well-defended foxhole. Limzy and I will keep watch over the house."

"I don't understand that defense," she responded and started walking.

"You shouldn't sit in the house. You have to go out and meet them."

"But they poisoned Mauzy. We already have one casualty. Isn't that enough?"

"That's why I'm with Limzy. That's the reason I'm going out with him."

When she drew closer and stood at his side, he saw how far her pregnancy had advanced. Her face had broadened, and it was as if her arms had pulled back and pushed out her belly. "You mustn't sit in the house. You have to go out and meet them.'' He repeated himself and immediately sensed that his words did not touch upon this meeting with her. They were the answer to some other question.

For a moment he forgot the fears and oppressions, and he spoke with a kind of youthful enthusiasm about the duty to guard the precious graves, because the vandals, Jew-haters, had one evil plan in mind: to destroy the Jews and expunge their memory from the face of the earth. Gad was stunned by his own voice for a moment. Amalia lowered her head, as though it were not her familiar brother speaking to her, the brother who had abandoned her at a hard time, but rather another brother, who had grown taller in a day and who had changed beyond recognition.

Gad put on his Uncle Arieh's fur coat and went out on watch. His eyes deceived him several times, and the night shadows looked like human figures, but Limzy didn't make any mistake. The dog lay quietly, curled up around his own body. From time to time he would straighten up, listen with heightened attention, and then curl up again. It seemed to Gad he wasn't guarding vigilantly enough, and he would wake him up and send him out into the darkness. Limzy would return promptly and curl up next to him. Amalia didn't come out. The front shutter was open, and Gad could see her sitting there. She sat by the stove and sipped drink after drink.

Now he saw his late Uncle Arieh standing by him, wearing the very coat Gad was wearing. Marvelous earthiness poured from his figure. He was a handsome man even in his latter days. More than anything, his shoulders, broad and straight shoulders like those of the mountain peasants, testified to that. At one time Gad asked Sophia whether Uncle Arieh had been with her. She denied it, but she did say that no true man went without a woman. The old men were fond of him, and more than once they blessed his memory. They repeatedly recalled that, were it not for him, for his courageous guardianship, the place would have been abandoned, and without a holy place there is no prayer. They did not speak about his righteousness or about his loyalty, but about his courage. That disturbed Gad somewhat, as though they were casting doubt upon his own courage.

Toward morning, slumber suddenly overtook him, but he overcame it and ran back to the house with Limzy. First he thought he would milk the cow and feed it, but he changed his mind and went inside. Amalia was still asleep. The smell of slivovitz and the odor of sweat stood in the room, and it was clear that if he didn't open the window now, the heavy odor would remain for many hours. He went over to the window and opened it.

Without opening her eyes, Amalia asked, "Who's there?"

"Me," Gad said and approached the couch.

"Who opened the curtains?"

"What curtains are you talking about?"

She sat up and supported herself on her arms, saying, "The curtains."

"You were dreaming. On the Plain we had curtains, not here."

Hearing that answer, she dropped her head back on the pillow like a girl who hadn't gotten what she wanted.

"You were dreaming. On the Plain we had curtains, not here," he repeated.

"I have a very bad headache," she said, without removing her head from the pillow.

"I opened the window," he said and walked over to it.

Amalia sank back into the pillow, and Gad went out, milked the cow, and gave it fodder. The cow was quiet, and Gad felt a hidden warmth for that mute beast which had lived by his side for years. For a long while he stood in the courtyard. Now he knew with a kind of clarity, as though after a great effort, that all he was fond of—the courtyard and all the tools: the sledgehammers, the pitchforks, the picks scattered about carelessly, which he and Amalia had used and, when necessary, repaired—all those mute souls would also remain for many days after he and Amalia were no longer there. Uncle Arieh had said several days before his death, "When the fruit of that tree ripens, I will no longer be here." Gad felt a kind of hidden and frightening closeness to the broad wooden casks that stood full of rainwater. The cow sometimes used to plunge its head in them and slurp the pure water. Limzy would also stretch out his front paws and lap it. The rainwater was Amalia's province. She used it for washing. Sunny days were also laundry days. She would bare her arms and immerse herself completely in the washbasin like a servant woman. Sometimes he would help her put up the clotheslines and hang out the wash. Her face next to the taut rope was that of a person happy with her lot.

Occasionally, at least on sunny days, a hint of jealousy would creep into his heart because she knew how to derive so much pleasure from her work, and he did everything in routine fashion, wearily, as though under compulsion. Only in time had he understood that she too lived with ups and downs. When she was on the rise, her face was bright like that of a young peasant woman, full of desire for life, happy and close not only to him but also to everything around her. But when she was depressed, which was frequently, her face was hidden behind a veil of darkness. He was scared then that she might alter and metamorphose into some other kind of creature. Those fears were vain. She would struggle with herself and finally be calmed. The light would return to her face. Now he saw the light in her face as he did not see it when it was truly lit up.

Meanwhile the sky was bare again, and the distant sun spread a pleasant warmth. He was tired from the night before, and yet he refused to heed his legs and go to bed. During the first years of their sojourn there, Amalia used to cut slices of golden russet apples and spread them out on mats in the sun to dry. Three or four days of sunlight would wrap the apple slices in a downy brown skin. Amalia used to make compotes out of the dried fruit, she baked them in corn pies, and sometimes she brought them to the table on large wooden platters. Now for some reason he remembered how she used to serve that fruit, with a kind of modest grace.

With the sun's death the light in her face died. She would wrap herself in blankets and seemingly announce that she was withdrawing from the world. Not all the winter days were gloomy. There were also hours of light. When her *malai* came out right, high and browned and full of the smell of fresh cheese, she would say, "The *malai* came out well," and the light of the summer would return to her face.

Now he was sorry the bright days were over and she would have to struggle with the little ghosts again. In the last few years he had clearly seen those dark creatures, a whole swarm of them, shapeless, like hairy lumps, plunging down and encircling her neck and her eyelids. Gad used to attack them furiously, and Amalia, hearing his shouts, would break out in a wild groan, as though warning him not to provoke them. These were the ghosts of winter, and more than anyone Amalia knew their oppressiveness. They plagued her with inordinate vehemence.

''Who's there?'' She woke up.

''Me.''

''I have a bad headache.''

''I opened the window. Do you want anything to drink?''

''No,'' she said and sank her head in the pillow. Gad took a chair and sat at some distance from her cot. His colorful daydreams shrank, and he knew for certain they would never return. A vague sadness, which he had borne with him all night long, spread through his chest. They had celebrated her thirty-first birthday by drinking too much. Extremely drunk, she had burst out in wild laughter and called herself an old maid who has no hope left except unnatural death. Gad wanted to silence her, but he too was drunk. Now the memory of the night was like yesterday.

Amalia, he wanted to call out, don't worry. I'll help you. We have come a good way, and we'll yet do a lot. No one will make us turn from this path. Through the good deeds of the multitude we too will be saved. Those were tired words that billowed up in his head.

She sank into sleep again. Her face was tense, and thin

shadows of winter gloom hovered over her eyelids. It occurred to him that a damp towel would relieve her. Their father also used to lay a damp towel on his head when headaches assailed him.

"Amalia," he said.

"What?"

"Wouldn't you like a damp towel?"

"No."

"A damp towel is good for headaches."

"I don't need anything," she said, and Gad knew that evil visions were preying upon her sleep, and their remnants were still floating in her head. They were pressing on her scalp and temples. The pillows were powerless to dissipate the pressure, and the pain grew stronger from moment to moment.

"Why are you being stubborn?" he said and shut his mouth.

CHAPTER 33

The next day her face was feverish, and she vomited and shivered. Gad wrapped her in three thick woolen blankets and said, "They'll warm you up, they have to warm you up." Several hours passed and they didn't warm her up. Gad stood by the burning stove, and in great desperation he cried out, "I don't know what to do. Everything I do is useless!"

If he had had a horse and wagon he would have gone down and brought up the medic. Two weeks after Uncle Arieh's death the horse had fallen down and died. It had been old, but its old age hadn't been evident, and when they took it out to pasture, it sometimes used to raise its head and rush off at a gallop. Uncle Arieh had been very fond of it and said, "Sunik is a human horse. He understands what people want, and he knows his way around the roads."

Since the horse's death, the cart had stood in the courtyard like a body with no soul. At one time Gad wanted to buy a horse in the village, but Amalia had been strictly opposed. She feared the horse would carry him to the gentile women too easily. The matter of the horse would come up now and then and quickly fade away. Once he told her, "You'll be sorry one day." But she was adamant: "I accept the responsibility."

"And if I get sick?" He wasn't afraid to speak bluntly.

"You mustn't think about that."

"What if we have to run away?"

"From On High we will be defended."

Thus she closed the issue. Gad was stunned by that firmness of resolve, but in his heart he knew that Amalia knew his secrets. The dream that toward evening he would mount the horse and gallop straight to Sophia's house, that dream, which he had secretly harbored for years, was nipped in the bud. In his heart he bore her a grudge because of that, but of course he didn't blame her openly.

The next day the fever did not abate, and she was still shivering. Gad tried to serve her tea by the spoonful, but she couldn't swallow the liquid, and he stood beside her bed, helpless, his shoulders narrowed.

In the evening a stream of words burst from her, words without any context, words only Gad could understand. For example, she suddenly called out, "You're not my mother, you're the store's mother. You're the Ruthenians' mother." Nor did Gad escape from her unscathed that evening. She called him "Sophia's beau."

He ignored her delirium and kept placing damp towels on her forehead day and night. For some reason he believed if he persisted she would calm down. That was merely a delusion. Heatedly she accused everyone who had shut her up in dark rooms, keeping her from the light of the sun and making false promises to her. She spoke a lot about Cimpulung, where their father had taken her when she caught pneumonia. She called the place the Garden of Light. For a moment she looked like that little timid Amalia who occasionally used to utter strange words, and whose mother used to hit her for that and insist that she speak in normal language, for otherwise people would think she was mentally handicapped. At moments of grace those unusual words would return to her here too and illuminate her face. Gad loved that face and would secretly keep watch for it, but now her mouth did not utter unusual words that she had collected in the store as a child but rather the words the Ruthenians used, harsh words that their mother used to say when she was angry. Strange, only one person escaped from her unscathed: Peter, the carpenter. That tall, pleasant gentile, of Polish origin, used to come twice a year to repair the shelves in the store, and once, on Passover eve, he brought four chairs with straw seats that immediately gave a feeling of newness to the house.

"What can I do?" He stood before her helplessly.

She answered with a barrage of words. Distant, repressed, forgotten matters rose up from the depths of the years and flooded her face, and it was clear there was no longer any connection between her and those years. Nevertheless they were feverish within her. This was typhus, and he knew it was typhus, and fear immobilized him. One evening while he was putting a damp cloth on her head, she called out in a voice not her own, "Why are they feeding me porridge? I hate porridge." That wasn't Amalia's voice but the voice of her older sister, Deborah, who had died of typhus as a child. She too, like Amalia now, had spouted feverish words, and their mother, desperate, had knelt down and said, "Child, I'm not giving you porridge. I'm putting a damp cloth on your head."

Now he regretted that during the summer, imprudently, he had brought many people into the house, old and sick people. Amalia had not objected. She had served the women submissively, like someone sated with sorrow, who had forgone her own desires and wanted only to be allowed to serve. Gad knew the people bore the dreadful plague but nevertheless had not kept a distance. He had been certain, for some reason, that the disease wouldn't harm them. Amalia's desire to help the people was also stronger than her fear or revulsion. She had slept in the same room with the women and served them coffee in the morning, and she had washed two old women with her own hands. Other fears had preoccupied Gad then: Amalia's pregnancy.

Meanwhile her face grew empty and her glance became dim. Beads of sweat glistened on her forehead with a frightening glint. Sometimes she would wake up in delirium and attack him with curses. That anger no longer hurt him. It seemed to him she was gradually overcoming the many enemies who were preying upon her. That too was an illusion. The disease grew stronger from hour to hour, and she would vomit every spoonful of tea he managed to feed her.

Now there was no alternative but to go down, and he decided to do so.

In the afternoon he went to the cemetery and asked forgiveness of the dead. He promised them: The moment Amalia got better, he would return and watch over them as before. A thin rain fell, and he returned to the courtyard and gave the cart a push. The cart, to his surprise, moved. He took off the wheels and smeared the axles with grease and tightened the brakes. The concentrated work made him forget Amalia's illness. For a moment it seemed to him it wasn't illness but a hallucination inspired by fear, and if he managed to uproot fear from her, the fever would also abate. When he finished the job he went inside and called out, "The cart is ready, and we are prepared to set out on our way." Amalia didn't react. Her breathing was labored, and her face was splotched with pale pink. Her big eyes were open, and fear sparkled from their pupils. Now she no longer spoke, but her muteness was blunter than any speech. It's my fault; he wanted to ask her pardon, but there was no need. She closed her eyelids tightly, and all at once her whole being was shrunken.

Then he left the courtyard, set the cow free, and sent it away. The cow was surprised and at first it refused to leave the barn. But finally it responded to his exhortations and turned aside with an insulted expression at being driven from its corner. Limzy whimpered with short barks, tucked his tail between his legs, and stepped to the side. Gad approached him and said, "Now you'll watch over the cemetery and the house. You mustn't be frightened. Fear is unseemly." Limzy bent his head as though he'd been scolded, and Gad kept on talking about Amalia, the poor thing, who was gripped by frightful hallucinations and fever. "I have to take her down to the medic. The trip will make her feel better, and I'm sure they won't hospitalize her. But meanwhile don't let anyone come near the house. Keep your eye on the cow too, because without her our lives are worth nothing,'' he said, and smiled as though he had caught the foolishness of his words. He considered taking vegetables and dairy products in the box in the back of the cart, but he gave up the idea and instead he shoved in two blankets, two pillows, and three bottles of slivovitz. He placed the strongbox full of money and jewels in the front. He pushed the cart up to the door of the house, cushioned the floor with two quilts, and, in his large arms, carried Amalia out and placed her inside. He went back and closed the door as though they were leaving on a short trip.

The cart was lighter than he had imagined. The brakes worked fine, and the downgrades weren't steep. Every hour or so he would stop the wagon, stick his head in, and look at her for a moment. Amalia didn't respond. Her face was sealed, and a thin film of darkness hovered over it.

After he had been pulling for some time, rain fell, and he took shelter under some oaks. Amalia's face opened up for a moment, and he told her that by now they'd made half the trip, and if everything went properly they would reach the medic by evening. The medic would examine her and give her medicine to relieve her fever. For some reason he expected her to react, but her face, though awake, didn't move.

When the rain stopped, he harnessed himself to the shafts and set out. Something told him he had to hurry, and indeed he gripped the shafts hard, took care to avoid the shoulders of the road, went around potholes, and braked well on down-grades. He managed the final steep section with his last strength. When he finally reached the river, his ankles were wounded, and his shirt was wet with sweat. But he did not delay. With the same determined breathing he pulled the cart to the medic's house.

The medic, who had lost something of his peasant look over the years, was surprised to see a man harnessed to a cart, and he said, "What's this here?" Gad slipped the rope from his shoulders, and without moving from his place he said, "My sister is very sick, sir."

"Let's see," said the medic.

Gad took off the covering and stepped aside. He expected that now the medic would lean over Amalia and examine her, but the medic didn't move. He stood at a distance, looked at her closed face, and said, "Yes, she's very sick."

"What am I to do, sir?" Gad asked in a lost voice.

"Straight to the hospital."

"Can't you do anything here? You have to give her some relief, don't you?" He spoke with a choked voice.

"What can I do? I'm only a medic," he said, and a crude smile spread across his face.

"Pardon me," said Gad, like someone who has been caught doing something foolish.

"You have to hire a wagon immediately." The medic spoke like an army military medic.

"Where is there any wagon? Where will I find one, sir?"

"We'll send the boy, and he'll bring a driver." He spoke like someone offering a tried-and-true remedy to some familiar ailment.

The boy set out at a dash, and for a moment Gad followed his run with his eyes. "Why isn't she talking?" he asked distractedly.

"The illness is at its peak," he declared, without further explanation.

"Isn't there any drug that will make her feel better?"

"There is, but only in the hospital. We medics don't have drugs like that." Now the peasant in him was talking, a mixture of ingenuousness and feigned ingenuousness. Gad knew that style of speech, and now he was frightened of him.

"Is the medicine there?"

"It certainly is." He spoke in a tone that sounded like a lie.

Gad looked again at Amalia's sealed face. "She's breathing heavily, isn't she?"

"That has to be taken care of too." He spoke in military fashion.

The driver was tardy, and Gad knew it wasn't an innocent delay. In times of trouble the drivers raise their prices, and if the patient is mortally ill they become exorbitant.

"Did you know my Uncle Arieh?" Gad spoke to him in a different tone.

"Certainly I knew him. He was a man of the great world."

" 'The great world,' you say?"

"Indeed. We would get information from him about everything that was happening in the world. Plenty of reliable information reached him. Are you his replacement?"

"I do my best."

"Once masses of pilgrims used to go up there."

"Now too," Gad said, for some reason.

Before long the driver appeared. The price he asked was close to that of a cow. Gad was stunned by the sum he demanded, and, very angrily, he said, "If a sword is pressed against your throat, you can't bargain."

"It's night, sir. Trips by night have a different price."

Gad went over to his cart, lifted up Amalia together with the quilts, and laid her in the peasant's wagon.

"Something in advance," demanded the peasant, and Gad gave him some money.

Gad had heard about the district hospital from the people who came up to the mountaintop. That was where they took patients who had to be isolated and those who had no hope of recovering from their illnesses. Gad now remembered they had also wanted to take his mother there, but his father had refused in a final act of desperation. No doubt that had hastened her death, but it had also spared her further affliction.

"When will we get there?" asked Gad.

"We never know God's will." The peasant's reply was not slow in coming.

"Have you been there often?"

"When necessary."

"How is it there?"

"We don't talk about it," he said curtly.

Now Gad regretted having taken the medic's advice. A sick person must first be returned to his native city and to the grave of his fathers, so that they, in their love, can pray for him.

"And there's no hope." The words left his mouth.

"Who said so?"

"I'm asking."

"You mustn't ask that way."

"You're right," said Gad, abashed.

Afterward he asked no more questions. Just once he asked to stop the wagon to look at Amalia. When the lantern light struck her face, her lips quivered and pursed. That was how her lips used to contract when dreams frightened her in her winter sleep. That piercing memory gave him hope that their journey through darkness would end with the light. When they had gone up to the mountaintop Amalia had also been sick and vomited, he remembered.

"Amalia," he called, "do you recognize me?" Amalia didn't respond. He called her again, and fear gripped his limbs. That was how their father had called their mother when she had closed her eyes.

From there on, the road became twisted and very bumpy, and fears and regrets filled his head. For a moment it seemed to him that the medic and the peasant had conspired to mislead him. But fatigue was greater than all else, and in the end he succumbed to it and fell asleep.

CHAPTER 35

As the darkness thinned, they reached the bank of the River Prut and the square in front of the hospital. Gad roused from his doze and asked, "Where are we?"

"We've arrived," said the peasant.

"Is this the district hospital?" Gad asked, as though he had been rehearsing the question.

"It and no other."

Dozens of wagons crowded around the low building. The smell of scorched milk and the odor of horse manure congealed in the morning darkness. The driver got off his wagon, put out his hand, and said, "The time has come to pay the rest."

Gad took silver coins out of his vest pocket and paid. The peasant counted and counted again, demanded more, and received it.

"What do we do now?" asked Gad, grasping his head with both hands.

"This is the hospital, and now my duty is done." The peasant tried to sound decent.

"Good Lord," Gad cried out. "I don't know what to do!" As he spoke, he overheard a conversation in Yiddish. A few people who were sitting in a wagon and a few others who were outside of it were arguing angrily. The argument was about a difficult decision, and no one was willing to bear the responsibility. Finally they consulted with an old man who was sitting deep inside the covered wagon, and he made the decision. The mutterings kept fluttering in the air, as after an argument with recriminations.

"Let's see who's standing at the entrance." The driver came to his assistance. Men and women were crowding around the gate at that time, putting out their hands and yelling loudly. It looked like the entrance of a prison on Tuesdays, when packages are delivered to the prisoners.

"There's nothing to be done. We have to wait," said the peasant in peasantlike tones.

"What will I do here alone?" Gad implored him.

"Everybody here is Jewish."

"I don't know anyone."

"You have to pay a bribe."

"To whom?"

"To the director."

"Do you know the director?"

"No, but the Jews know him."

"Just wait with me for another hour until the sun rises," said Gad, handing him two more pieces of silver.

The peasant didn't bargain.

Gad tried to find out from people in the neighboring wagons when and how new patients were accepted. "All the places are taken. There's a line of hundreds. They don't bring in anyone new until a patient dies," they told him.

"I'm going away," he told the peasant absentmindedly.

"Where?"

"Home."

For a moment he saw the gate again. A robust guard was standing in the entrance, and with both arms he was pushing away the people who were trying to approach him. Imprecations flew in every direction, and the guard threatened that if they didn't step back he would call the gendarmes.

"Is it like this all the time here?" he asked the peasant awkwardly.

"Bribery solves every problem."

"But who do you give the bribes to?" Gad spoke like a storekeeper.

"I'll go in by the back door. Sometimes you find the right man there," said the peasant and walked away.

Gad didn't move. A cup of coffee. Isn't there a cup of coffee in this whole place? An old morning yearning was roused within him. Years ago, when he was still a boy, his father had taken him to the hospital to have his infected tonsils removed. Then too it had been a purplish morning like this, and his father himself had shivered in the morning chill. He had spoken with the kind of words he normally didn't use. He spoke about the need to remove the evil from the body and to purify it of harmful illnesses. Many people were bustling about, and wagons loaded with sacks and people stood as if they had been there forever. The boy, who had stifled his fear for a long time, burst out in bitter tears, and the father hugged him and promised him it wouldn't hurt much and everything would be over in a jiffy. But the boy's fears were stronger than the father's assurances, and he cried and begged, "Not now, not today!" Since his comforting words had been useless, the father scolded the boy out loud and told him then that everyone suffers, and there are dreadful illnesses and harsh pains, and you mustn't indulge yourself in this world, because this world lasts only the wink of an eye, and truth and righteousness come to us in the world of truth. But those words hadn't soothed the boy's fears, and he kept on crying as though he had just learned that the world was an abyss and in a short while he would be thrown down its maw.

During the long wait, the boy became reconciled to the thought that in a moment the abyss would yawn and he would be devoured. The father grasped the boy's trembling hand and promised him again that it wouldn't hurt much. When the doctor's door finally opened, the blue walls had suddenly sparkled in a damp light, and he had tried to flee. His father had seized him with both his hands, which were so lean they seemed not like hands but tongs. The doctor, an old man whose long eyebrows shaded small benevolent eyes, ordered him to open his mouth. He looked and looked again and said softly, "There's no need to hurry. Why rush? Let's wait a month or two and see." So instead of tying him down, putting him to sleep, and removing the tonsils, he wrote the name of some medicine and that of a pharmacist on a white slip of paper. For that good advice he asked only a few pennies. "Redemption comes in the wink of an eye," said his father when they had gone out the doctor's door. That was also an indirect reproach to himself for not believing and for giving himself over to despair. The boy was greatly relieved. He cried with a different kind of tears until he fell asleep in his father's arms. From that nightmare only a small scar was left, which would suddenly wake him in the darkness and remind him that the wound was not completely healed.

Meanwhile the peasant came back and said, "It's very crowded. The guards are hitting people mercilessly."

"What shall we do?" Gad raised his eyes to the peasant.

"Not far away there's a private hospital. Maybe they can take her there."

"Will you go with me?"

"If you pay."

Gad handed him some silver coins. The peasant counted them, narrowed his eyes, made a calculation, and said, "It's not worth my while, but I'll do it for the sake of the *mitzvah*." Gad was surprised by the peasant's voice, by the way he used that Jewish word and pronounced it correctly.

"You know the Jews well, I see."

"To a certain extent."

"You worked for them?"

"When I was young I used to transport their wares. They always paid the price we agreed upon, but once a merchant cheated me. He ran away without paying. Since then I won't move until I've been paid."

"That's wise," said Gad.

"People are known to be sinners, isn't that so?"

They drove south, and Gad was glad he had found the right peasant to ramble about with. For a moment he wanted to thank him, but he immediately remembered that the peasant would interpret that as a weakness and ask for more money. Amalia neither opened her eyes nor uttered a sound. He touched her arm and called, "Amalia. I'm by your side." She gave out a rasp that sounded like a groan. "That's a good sign, isn't it?" he asked the peasant.

"It would seem so," he answered. Now he noticed that the peasant never committed himself to a definite opinion. For a moment he was astonished by that wisdom, but he immediately grasped that it wasn't ingenuous.

After a two-hour journey he stopped at an inn. They had a few drinks, and the peasant expressed his opinion: "You know how to drink. Jews usually don't know. But you do." It was an old-fashioned tavern where Jews never stop. The sweat of animals and the smell of ground corn stood in the air. They sat in the open courtyard. The morning had spread out in its glory, full and chilly. Gad suddenly saw the mountaintop before his eyes. He hid his head in his hands and knew that now the peasants were looting the house. Before that they had scattered poisoned meat and killed Limzy. They had brought the cow down to be slaughtered. I have to go back, to go back at once! he wanted to shout, but his voice remained imprisoned in his throat. Still, the words "go back" escaped his mouth.

The peasant raised his eyes, surprised. "Go back where?"

"I was mistaken." He recovered his wits. "Let's go on. Do we still have a long way?"

"An hour or two."

"Thank the Lord."

"Among us, we never give thanks until things are all over," the peasant corrected him.

They advanced along the Prut, and the peasant wasn't content. The Jews always made him go out of his way. Money can't solve everything. There are things more important than money. Life is more important than property. Only the Jews are never sated with money. He was drunk, and the words flowed from his mouth. Gad forgot his distress for a moment and looked at him. He had known peasants like that from his childhood, but the years on the mountaintop had made him forget their faces. Now he looked at him as though he were recounting wonders to him.

"Is it a long way?" asked Gad.

"Don't ask."

"Why not?"

"Because that makes the way longer."

The strange reason amused Gad, and he chuckled. The

peasant looked at him scornfully and said, "Jews laugh at everything. Everything strikes them funny."

Later he sobered up and his mood improved. Gad asked him to stop the wagon. Amalia's face was exposed as though it were floating on the covers that wrapped her. "Amalia," he called. "I'm by your side." He put his hand on her forehead. "She has no fever, it seems to me. Maybe I'm wrong."

They started out again. The peasant told him that once the hospital had been famous, and it was called Dr. Marcus's Hospital. People used to come from the whole region, and of course a lot of Jews. The peasant's moderate voice blunted Gad's fears for a moment, and he said to himself, Now she's asleep. Sleep is good for her. Sleep will cure her. Those weren't his own words. Apparently he had absorbed them during his childhood, or perhaps on the mountaintop. Relief poured down the length of his body, and he was glad he was doing his duty without shirking. As they continued along the banks of the Prut, Gad raised his eyes, and the mountaintop was revealed in its full earthliness, a gigantic boulder rising up among the mountains, shaped like a wild mushroom.

"Is that the mountaintop?" asked Gad with a blocked voice.

"That and no other."

"Is that how it looks from here?"

"Do you live there?"

"All year around."

"Do the Jews still go up there?"

"They do."

"Once, I remember, a lot of them used to climb the trails."

"Fewer now."

That short conversation brought the vision of the mountaintop before his eyes in all its concreteness, green and in its full clarity, as though the rain had purified it. Within that green sea stood Amalia. She put her hand on the abandoned cart in the courtyard, and the look on her face was that of a person who feels remorse. Ever since the horse had died she was depressed. It was forbidden to mourn for animals. Even for people it is forbidden to mourn excessively. He scolded her. When the big acacia tree collapsed she had also mourned for it. For days she would say repeatedly, "The snow killed it." Only then did he grasp that her life was unlike his. Her contacts with objects and animals were different. He realized it, but it was hard for him to admit it.

Meanwhile he roused and asked out loud, "Where are we?"

"We've arrived," said the peasant.

"I don't see anything."

Behind the oaks stood a low building, surrounded by wagons, huts, and a few bonfires that sent up thick smoke.

"It's all full," said Gad.

"We'll overcome that obstacle too. You mustn't give up hope." The peasant's moderate, self-righteous voice had returned.

"Correct," said Gad, without noticing what had left his mouth. Only now did he sense that he was in the midst of a nightmare. His legs were tied, and if he were required to walk, he would be unable to take even a single step.

"Amalia," he called out.

"What do you want from her? You mustn't wake her up."

"Correct."

"I'll go and see who's at the gate."

The moment the peasant expressed that intention, Gad realized he had made a grave error, an error that could not be corrected but only atoned for. But what was that error, and how could he atone for it? He didn't know. The cold lights of the night lit up the clearing. The place looked like a Gypsy encampment, full of hubbub and crammed with children. They were talking Ukrainian, the Ukrainian of the mountains, Sophia's language. "I understand that language. I can express myself in that language," he said, as though he had been asked.

"They want a bribe." The peasant returned with news.

"How much."

"Five thousand, no less."

"If I have to, I'll sell the house," said Gad, careful about what he was saying. He would never let the driver know how much cash he had in his pockets, for fear he would rob him on the way.

"What house are you talking about?" the peasant asked in surprise.

"What do you mean? The house on the mountaintop. It has four spacious rooms, a kitchen, a woodshed, and a cellar. Nothing's lacking there."

"And who'll watch over the graves?" The peasant surprised him.

"To save a life you can break the sabbath, as the Jews say." Hardly had he said those words when he realized that once he had wanted to send Amalia back to Zhadova, and he had even offered her the inheritance that Uncle Arieh had left them, but his motive wasn't pure, and she had refused. Her face had been clear that evening, and her look had implored him, Don't trick me. Why are you tricking me? Cheating disgusts me.

Night fell, and Gad approached one of the wagons to ask, "When do they take in new patients?"

"They don't take in a new patient unless someone dies."

"Everywhere it's the same thing." Something of the peasant stranger's voice clung to him.

"Are there Jews here?" he continued asking, for some reason.

"There certainly are. You can find them everywhere," said the peasant and turned his back to him.

Hardly had he moved away from the Ruthenian when a cold torrent sliced down his spine, gripped his knee joints, and spread over his legs. His feet were heavy as though they were cast in metal. "What's this?" he said to himself. "I should have taken a scarf. Without a scarf you can easily catch a chill."

The driver returned with only a single word: cash. Only for cash could something be done. Gad knew it was a plot. If he entrusted the jewels to the peasant, he would run away.

"I have a house. I'm willing to give you the house." Gad raised his voice.

"Here you need cash. Without cash no one will let her in." He spoke cunningly from the throat.

"I have a fifty note. That's all I have."

"There's nothing even to talk about. I'm going back home. You can't depend on Jews."

"You can't leave a person in an open field." Gad spoke to him in his own dialect.

"This isn't an open field. There are people here."

Now Gad felt weakness spreading over his whole body. He gripped the edge of the wagon and said, "Take me home. I'll pay you double and twice over."

"What are you talking about?"

"Take me to Zhadova. It's not far from here. I can't bear this blow."

The peasant's face turned red, and anger flooded his features. "You tricked me. You told me that you'd put her in the hospital here, so we brought her here. I found a guard who is willing to let her in, and now you change your mind and want to go home." Now it was clear he had been plotting to steal the jewels, but because the scheme hadn't succeeded, he was angry. "The Jews are cheaters, always cheaters."

"I'll give you this watch." Gad tried to cut off his anger. "It's an expensive watch, pure silver. If you take me to Zhadova, it will be yours. This watch is worth a fortune."

"I don't need watches."

"You won't find watches like this one anymore, a work of art. If we leave now, we'll be in Zhadova by midnight." Weakness frothed in his legs, but he didn't let up. As though it were a wonder, he showed him how valuable the watch was: you could buy a cow for it.

His words had their effect. The watch charmed the driver, and he agreed on condition that he receive the watch immediately. "Now I'll give you the money"—Gad found a way of outwitting him—"and when we get to Zhadova I'll give you the watch."

"The Jews always mix me up. I won't drive on until I have the watch in my hand." Gad also overcame that resistance. He added a small pearl-handled pocketknife to the money, and the peasant agreed. Amalia's face was sunk in sleep. A few yellow patches clung to her forehead. Gad recognized those patches, and for some reason he saw them as a good sign.

Later, already prostrate at Amalia's feet, rocked by the rutted, unpaved road, he knew the chill wasn't a cold. That was the way Amalia had shivered before she had fallen into deep sleep.

A quiet evening spread over the green fields, and the horses ambled along lazily. Gad now remembered that many years ago, while he was still a little boy, he had been sick and burning with a high fever. His father had taken him to the medic to decide whether he had to be hospitalized. They had traveled in a wagon lined with straw. His father was very tired from his fear and from his irritation, and he had fallen fast asleep. The boy was suddenly frightened by his father's sleep, and he had burst out in a shout. The father had been very alarmed and, not knowing what he was doing, he had slapped his face. That distant recollection, which had been buried in his memory, made him very happy, as if his father were standing some distance from him with his arms held open toward him.

"Driver," he called out.

"What's the matter?"

"Nothing. It seemed you had fallen asleep."

From then on his memory was burning but clear, like a globe of blown glass expanding with every breath. The long fish of the Prut appeared to him again. In dry years they used to lift their heads up out of the water and beg to be saved. The next day one would find them thrown up on the bank, their mouths open, their fins muddied, with despair floating in their dead eyes.

The evening twilight lasted a long time, and he saw the years on the mountaintop as though they were spread out on a carpet of green fire. It seemed to him he heard Amalia's voice saying, Why don't we have a drink? I need a drink like air to breathe. At one time those demands used to frighten him like the way she hugged Mauzy and Limzy. But in the last years he had become accustomed to them. More than that, he looked forward to them. During the past year, sometimes, after a drink, he had fallen upon her and stripped off her clothes the way you peel the skin off a cooked vegetable. The memory of her naked body flickered before his eyes as though borne on the waves of the evening.

Afterward his memory narrowed, and he no longer saw anything. The pain was strong, and his fever was high. But the feeling that he was suffering from the same illness and burning with the same fever dispelled his fears. He curled up at her feet and let his head sink down in the straw.

ABOUT THE AUTHOR

Aharon Appelfeld was eight when he witnessed the murder of his mother by the Nazis. After escaping from a concentration camp, he wandered in the forests for two years. When the war ended he joined the Soviet Army as a kitchen boy, eventually emigrating to Palestine in 1946. The author of eleven internationally acclaimed novels, including *Badenheim 1939, The Age of Wonders, Tzili, To the Land of the Cattails*, and *Katerina*, he lives in Jerusalem.